IN AND OUT
OF THE
GOLDFISH BOWL

LIBRARY OF WALES

Rachel Trezise's debut novel *In and Out of the Goldfish Bowl* won an Orange Futures Award in 2001. Her short story collection *Fresh Apples* won the inaugural International Dylan Thomas Prize in 2006. Her second story collection *Cosmic Latte* won the Edge Hill Prize Readers' Award in 2014. Her first play *Tonypandemonium* was staged by National Theatre Wales in 2013 and won the Theatre Critics of Wales Award for Best Production. Her play, *We're Still Here* premiered in 2017. She lives in the Rhondda.

IN AND OUT
OF THE
GOLDFISH BOWL

RACHEL TREZISE

PARTHIAN
LIBRARY OF WALES

Parthian, Cardigan SA43 1ED
www.parthianbooks.com
The Library of Wales is a Welsh Government initiative which
highlights and celebrates Wales' literary heritage in the English language.
Published with the financial support of the Welsh Books Council.
www.thelibraryofwales.com
Series Editor: Dai Smith
First published in 2000
© Rachel Trezise, 2000
© Foreword, Carolyn Hitt
Library of Wales edition published 2017
ISBN: 978-1-912109-79-1
Cover art: Face in Colour (Paint/oil pastel) by Bronwen Lewis
Typeset by Elaine Sharples
Printed in EU by Pulsio SARL

Years go by will I choke on my tears
till finally there is nothing left
one more casualty you know we're too
EASY easy easy

Tori Amos
'Silent All These Years'
from Little Earthquakes

FOREWORD

Before Rachel Trezise there were two things I'd never experienced in my home valley. One, a female literary voice from the Rhondda. Two, a writer who dared to expose the darkness, dysfunction and despair that can exist beneath the warm clichés of community life to which we still cling.

It was an uncomfortable yet entirely necessary epiphany. Here was I, a valley girl contentedly exiled in Cardiff, reflecting on the Rhondda at arm's length. Proud of its past. Unwilling to concede some of the more difficult realties of its present.

My Rhondda was steeped in the nostalgia of family history. Not that these tales were cute and cosy, of course. The miner grandfathers I never knew, both dead in their 50s – one claimed by dust, the other paralysed in a pit accident. The grandmother who saw four of her twelve children die before their sixth birthday and whose life was consumed by the relentlessness of domestic toil.

But our Rhondda narrative was selective. It was built on looking backwards at the nobility of the men and women who endured that hardship and saw education as the escape shaft and community kinship as their survival strategy.

When I was growing up in 1970s Llwynypia, there was a book on my parents' shelf that explored these valleys values and shaped my rear-view-mirror perspective. Called *Rhondda Past and Present*, this large tome had a poignant picture of a coal-covered 12-year-old collier on the dust jacket and contained twelve essays and a letter to the then Secretary of State for Wales.

Entirely written by men, the essays had grown out of a series of lectures held in the early 1970s at the new Treorchy comprehensive – where Rachel would be a pupil two decades later. Though the title said *Rhondda Past and Future*, the division was not equal. The book was dominated by history rather than current affairs.

As the introduction stated, the lectures tried to capture the detail of "that Rhondda experience, the long bitterness of the Depression, the struggle between worker and capitalist, the place of the chapel and choral singing, the clash of politics, the stubborn fight to provide secondary schools, the influence of the Workmen's Institutes, the humour, the pride, the compassion of ordinary people."

Only the final two chapters grappled with the challenges of post-industrial valley life. And though the essay entitled "Planning a Future for Rhondda's People" outlined some stark statistics on unemployment, deprivation and a growing housing crisis, there was still a reluctance to articulate the inevitable social problems such factors caused.

The sensitivity of the author in the face of outside criticism was clear: "The television programmes on the Rhondda tend to over-emphasise the deprived nature of the community – they show streams that have old cars in them rather than those that have not. They show the worst of the old housing rather than the best. They stress the worst of the community life rather than the best."

Yet the final sentence of the book – coming as it does after more than 200 pages of nostalgic Rhondda pride – was devastating in its desperation: "The Valleys and their way of life, their community feeling, their short but very human history, are an essential part of the character and tradition of Wales. The Valleys are dying. Wales will not be the same without them."

In 1978, three years after those words were written, Rachel Trezise was born into that troubled and changing Rhondda. And if the pay-off of that book on my parents' shelf was a cry for help, the semi-autobiographical novel Rachel crafted from the desolate experiences of her valleys childhood and youth is a roar of rage.

In and Out of the Goldfish Bowl is unflinching in its portrayal of a young girl growing up in a family fractured by domestic violence, alcohol and drug dependency and child abuse. The first-person narrative traces the story of Rebecca Trigianni as she attempts to navigate childhood and adolescence with an alcoholic mother, an absent abusive father and a step-father who subjects her to repeated sexual assaults.

Raw, visceral and brutal, the novel moves beyond its complex protagonist's interior monologue to examine the difficulties of another character – the Rhondda itself. We see not so much the scars of industrial decline but the open wounds inflicted on those who struggle with the socio-economic problems of the 1990s.

It may be Cool Cymru in Cardiff, but there is no sense of a confident post-devolution dawn at the other end of the valley line.

But just like that other great Rhondda writer Gwyn Thomas, Rachel can still extract laughter from the dark. Her exploration of taboo topics is made all the more powerful by the dry and waspish valleys wit that undercuts it. There is tenderness and poignancy too.

Yet most of all there is honesty and courage. Here is a young woman's voice telling a story many would prefer had remained untold because it is not valleys life as we would like to see it. *In and Out of the Goldfish Bowl* doesn't just remove our rose-tinted Rhondda spectacles, it rips them off and smashes them underfoot.

In doing so it provides a lesson to the rest of Wales. How often do we seek to celebrate our successes with blind patriotism rather than scrutinise our failures with mature and considered analysis?

Those who cannot cope with Trezise's Rhondda should not be blinded simply by the shock value of In and Out of the Goldfish Bowl. It is far more nuanced than that. For, ultimately, this is a survival story that draws on the resilience and defiance that have defined the Rhondda of the past *and* the present.

I may have romanticised the valleys values of my grandparents' generation but there is nothing corny or clichéd about the strength of character the females who came before me displayed and hopefully passed on – a strength I still perceive as a particular Rhondda trait.

And in this novel, as Rebecca attempts to overcome the traumas of her upbringing, it is female power that proves pivotal. We see the terminally-ill grandmother – a traditional valleys woman – pass on her "gift-wrapped" strength to her granddaughter.

It is the moment when the Rhondda of the past meets the Rhondda of the present. And, as Rachel Trezise's groundbreaking fiction demonstrates, we need to appreciate both if we are to understand the Rhondda of the future.

Carolyn Hitt

IN AND OUT
OF THE
GOLDFISH BOWL

1

My mother's bedroom was always cheerfully lit with a big bright lamp, the shade gathered prettily and adorned with lace. Homemade, as were most of the soft furnishings. Her clumsy grey plastic record player conditioned the air with the warped vinyl sounds of Tom Jones or Dolly Parton. We'd sit together in front of her lengthy mirror and sing the songs of happiness we'd heard so many times before. At the time Dolly Parton singing about prostitution and Kenny Rogers crooning over some broken marriage seemed perfectly natural, songs to be happy about and join in with. I would watch my mother with admiration as she dressed in silk frocks almost as beautiful as herself, painted the lids of her eyes with some glittering cosmetic and gained height with six-inch stilettos. It was autumn and I was a year older when she curled her hair around some hot pink cylinders. We listened as a dull cursing became audible from downstairs.

My father's voice, deep as it was, increased in volume as he folded up the white and fawn coney-fur coats he'd bought for my mother over the past seventeen years and clumsily pushed them into the Parker fire. He stabbed them, one by one, with the poker. His aim was faulty and I shuddered each time the poker scraped against the metal fire front. The racket filled me (just turned four) with all the fear of seeing a teacher run her oversized fingernails down an unspoiled blackboard. This was louder; I wasn't surrounded by desks and schoolchildren; this was happening in my home and it wasn't a fat woman wearing thick brown tights posing a threat. It was my father.

Returning to the bedroom I watched stupefied and silently inquisitive as tears fell rapidly from my mother's eyes, spoiling

1

her carefully placed make-up on their way and landing in the breast of my fourteen-year-old brother who comforted her as I stood alone in what seemed like anarchy.

It looked as though I had been born into a siding. My mother, James and I always in one place and my father in another. The marriage of Susan and Ray Trigianni had begun to dysfunction. A limit to a twenty-year-old devotion with a big stigma of awkwardness attached to it became visible, even to my rhymeless young self.

A couple of days later when I arrived home from school I approached the front door as my father emerged. He failed to acknowledge me and rushed to his car. My mother appeared, particularly fragile, red-faced and laden with fresh tears. As my father sat in his car, crashing doors and shouting in our direction, my mother picked up the empty milk bottles from the doorstep and hurled them at the car, one after the other. They both missed the then-moving car and landed on the grass at the other side of the road. One smashed against the frostbitten ground. I watched as blankly and as perplexed as the first time I had seen my mother cry. She lit a cigarette. That would be the last time I would see my father for a long time.

I scarcely acknowledged the absence of my father. As far as I could comprehend, James, my mother and I lived in the same house, we ate the same food, my mother was still beautiful and that seemed like all I needed to continue living a normal life.

It seemed wholly natural to me that my biological parents were no longer together. All mothers and fathers broke up, didn't they? To see mums and dads together picking up their children from nursery caused me a terrible unfamiliarity or a piercing jealousy. I was never sure which. The trauma of divorce was said to affect James much more than me: after all, he'd known our father ten years longer than I had and was old enough to be told or to figure out exactly what had gone on and why. Things I didn't have the comfort (or perhaps the discomfort) of understanding.

2

I wonder what effect my parents' divorce actually had on me. Surely it's not mentally healthy to be born smack into a milk bottle fight, but to be brutally honest I've never given a shit. They were separated, divorced and my father had been missing for a year before I was five. I was left only with brief muffled memories of my father ever being in the house. One time: it's Christmas Eve and we're only now trimming up. My mother and I are on our knees untangling lights and my father is decorating the tree. They are all short moments of vision, they are all devoid of dialogue. Another time: my brother and I are in a boat with our father, sailing across some mud-filled Porthcawl or Barry Island lake. Intent (as always) on gaining someone's attention, I've removed my shoes and for some reason my white ankle-socks and I'm balancing on the side of the boat, one leg being held by my brother and the other in the water, threatening to jump for no good reason. Even here my mind is concentrated more on my chubby toes dipped into the freezing brown water than with my father rowing frantically in order to get back before I actually do jump. There are others, of course, but all equally basic. Polaroid photographs which my imagination has added to.

It's almost as though I was born single parently. The only difference being the mystique of not knowing whether there's a caring father out there somewhere. I know there's not.

James's reaction to the blow was to throw himself into his O levels and his newly found job at Billy Granville's garage in Hendrefadog. From the time he was five years old he lived for cars, toy ones that he could pull apart and put back together. He got his first real car at the age of thirteen. A shell of a Capri which sat in the garden for four years while he slowly but surely transformed it into a brand-new gleaming red thing. His Saturday money maker turned into a fully fledged apprenticeship as a panel beater and sprayer even though he passed most of his exams and his teachers pleaded with him to stay at school. He left every morning at 6 am, returned every evening at 8 pm, worked Sundays, bank and public holidays. While most people work to cope with the cost of living, James seemed to need physical labour to live. What began as an antidote to home problems turned into a fully acquired dependency.

He was wrapped inside the UK punk movement and his tall, teenage meagre body fitted under no doorway in the house, while his sliced thin legs clad in skin-tight bleached denim seemed to be the attraction of every girl in the street who listened to The Clash, the Pistols or the UK Subs. When he wasn't at work his brash musical friends filled my evenings with gaiety and frivolity, constantly strummed guitars, and hit a vivid red drum kit James had bought with his first earnings. My mother seemed to be no different in age from the adolescents who kept a brilliant party on-going in our house. She rode the motorbikes, played the drums and drank the drink. While she waited on clubgoers at Polikoff's every evening, James and his array of colourful friends were expected to baby-sit. Boys and horror films. It's difficult to imagine a child's first dealings with life, a world so ruled by innocence, fresh emotion and unwrapped feelings. I harboured deep excitement in my new tastes of life.

If I could have seen through the disguise a mother tends to wear in her child's presence, I wonder if I would have felt a little different. I wonder if I would have started to feel the guilt seeping in there and then. The guilt that would eventually hit me at some place or some time or another.

My mother was holding down three jobs. A barmaid in a club, a barmaid in a pub, and a Saturday frozen food market trade assistant, all in order to feed me and put shoes on my feet. Between trying to pay electricity and solicitor's bills, she was having to sacrifice buying cigarettes to get bread on the table. The late-night phone calls from Father Christmas were actually nuisance calls, probably from my father, and eventually got so frustrating that my mother paid considerable amounts to change our number, numerous times.

The telephone was the most vivid, memorable thing from that

4

house. I would watch my mother sitting cross-legged on the black leather cushion with the lime-coloured receiver stuck to her face. It was all those times when she would be speaking to some receptionist or solicitor, I would wonder who the hell the woman was. It was also where I learned to spell my name. She spelt it out so much I began to repeat it faster and clearer until it rolled off my tongue in the most eloquent and natural state. Trigianni. T-R-EYE-G-EYE-A-DoubleN-EYE.

My mother seemed to me like a bird with a broken wing. The free spirit who loved country music and sherry, who could fly off on her push-bike or motorbike and find a life anywhere for herself, she was so beautiful and fun-loving. But she had me, her broken wing. She was fully aware of this ailment so mostly I stayed quiet and well-behaved. When I needed or occasionally wanted her attention I screamed and she would feel a pain on one side of her body and know that she couldn't fly off and leave her baby. When she was talking to all these strangers I knew I could shout or run to her and these strangers would know that I was more important to her right then.

Many of my mother's boyfriends came and went. They meant nothing to me and little to my mother, but one she brought home visited more than any of the others, and stayed sometimes for weeks on end. Brian was a tall, pale man with dark hair and stubble. My mother seemed very fond of him. He in return evidently loved my mother. If a marriage was going to come of it I much favoured the boyfriend she had had before because he was a book illustrator, and would sit for hours showing me photographs, drawings and cartoons of animals, asking me which one should go into the next book. Each time he arrived at the house he would offer me chocolates and some kind of spirit for my mother. He was eleven years younger than my mother with flaxen hair and smart clothes. With a pencil in his hand he was weighed down with my art requests. He'd translate my long ginger plaits and cheeky child features into sketches and cartoons which always carried a wicked witch theme. There were portraits of my brother and mother in delicate charcoals which my mother would put into her suitcase under the bed. The sacred paper box containing our birth certificates, her divorce papers, postcards from the family and a massive collection of Christmas and birthday greetings.

The idea of my mother marrying a living, breathing artist was acutely exciting, but for reasons I expect only my inscrutable mother knew, she selected Brian Williams, the professional miner and amateur fisherman.

2

I was seven years of age the next time I saw my father. We were living in a street called Lower Terrace in a village called Hendrefadog. It was a street of segregation, the left side littered with council properties and the right terraced with private houses. We lived in number 54, the left side. Every house on our side was identical. Pebble-dashed an ugly orange, brown and white, with a fence of rotting green wood surround and a front door with a square, corrugated lead-graphed glass at eye-level. A dirty brown river rushed past our garden. If you followed our pebble-dash-littered path to the end of our garden, you would be separated from the river only by an overgrown hedge. Nightmares based on a zombie extending from the river, arms outstretched, draped in seaweed and exuding an unpleasant piscine odour, like some sort of evil impersonating Jesus, plagued most of my living there.

Brian had taken the pseudonym of 'Dad' long before he had married my mother in Pontypridd Register Office, a few months after we moved to Hendrefadog. James still occupied a bedroom in our house but sightings were rare. I saw him at breakfast on school days, and those moments were not favourable for him or for me. He woke in an abominable mood if it had to be before 10 am. Years of early mornings and late nights had taken their toll on my brother's energy and moods. Mammy would butter toast for me, pour tea for herself and put a clean ashtray on the table for James. The kitchen was regularly described as not having enough room to swing a cat, and each time my six-foot brother stood up his head would hit the ceiling with enough force to dent it. I was convinced that one day his head would crash through and stick like a hair-dressing doll with no body, just a head, smeared with mascara on the floor of the upstairs landing. Each time he would let out a high-pitched swearword and press down his shovel-like hands on top of his head as if to stop the pain escaping from the top. If Mammy's eyes were securely fixed on burnt toast I would smirk silently at him and he would return a slovenly Johnny Rotten jib before slamming the door behind him.

I became unhealthily obsessed in Lower Terrace with cleaning. At seven years old I had never been asked to wash a cup. I did voluntarily wash a whole set of dinner crockery once but James had complained later that all his food tasted of Imperial Leather. I had no interest in the subject and all housework was something invented purely for mothers, so I will never know exactly how it originated.

Every morning I emerged from the house armed with dustpan and hand-brush and began sweeping the stones from the road into the kerb and later threw them in the river, where they were completely out of sight. I put my thin but entire energy into making the road totally smooth. I felt so strongly about the subject, that I once threw one of the stones at a boy because he had kicked some stones out of place. I closed my eyes and aimed, expecting to miss but opened my eyes instead to find Philip Burnelle on the floor, covered in blood.

It was on one of these dusty Sunday cleaning crusades that I met my natural father.

Having completed the bottom half of the terrace, I had to wait at the pavement for a car to pull up. This was a common practice. The noisy-wheeled green vehicle stopped beside me and I started back to the gate to watch a tall, dark stranger walk towards me. He had already handed me a pink teddy bear and greeted me before I squinted my eyes and realised it was my father. That man. I ran, closed the gate behind me and flew into the living room where my Dad was watching television. I clung to him as tears seeped from my eyes. My mother handled the incident.

Four years can cause a child to forget so much. Not a letter or a Christmas card passed my way. His name was hardly mentioned, at least not in my presence. Although, sometimes my mother would pose a peculiar question which went simply along the lines of, 'You don't care about your father, do you, Rebecca?' I answered automatically, 'No, of course not,' because that seemed to make my mother happy and I never thought about him enough to make a real decision. 'No, you love Daddy, don't you? Good girl.'

My body at the time of this incident was filled from head to toe with awe. Perhaps because I really didn't care about this man, perhaps because I had been conditioned to feel this way. However, this foreigner who had caused me to be here I regarded with dread and my now real father, the amateur fisherman, I regarded as safety. I refused to speak to the threatening figure whose face would be as unmemorable the next morning as it had been for the past four years. After thirty minutes he left and relieving normality resumed.

Something which struck me in these still tender years about myself was that nothing really did seem normal. I just didn't seem normal. My mother told me that I was an exceptionally intelligent child, but this abnormality had nothing to do with talent or intelligence, because I knew that I could read more than the other kids, draw prettier pictures and had started writing stories about the unacceptability of cruelty to animals; it's just that sometimes I would say something in the classroom that not even the teachers could understand. My mother told me around this point that one day, when I was eighteen months old and my brother ten years old, he had looked out of the window and admired the sunset, but I had tapped him on the shoulder, held his face to mine and said, 'That's not the sun. That's a big yellow bomb.'

The statement was followed in later months with an entire story of how my name wasn't Rebeeca, it was Rosemary, I wasn't a baby, I was thirty-eight years old and expecting a baby, my husband David was away at World War II, and I feared a bomb might kill me. This sparked a new suspicion about myself. How could a perfectly normal child come up with stuff like this when she hadn't long learned how to talk? And on that subject I remembered my first words. Not so much words as speech. 'Mum' or 'Dad' being just too normal for me, I had to go and recite the entire 'Little Piggy' nursery rhyme. There I was lying in my cot talking of markets and roast beef, before I had learned my mother's name. I heard my mother telling a neighbour once that the first time a social worker called to see if I was developing properly, I had been in a baby bath in front of the fire. As she asked my mother if I was completing adequate sentences, I got out of the bath, walked to the woman, pointed to the window and said, 'Look at it out there, it's pissing down.'

My mother described these happenings as remarkable while I began to distress myself with fears of who I was. There were many possibilities but 'ordinary' was not one. Such thoughts began to set a tone of isolation for my life. Of course it was not this alone; my insecurity was to gather many more helping hands along the way, but I know it is this that started the ball rolling, the boulder that would eventually render me utterly useless.

All my belongings, toys, clothes and things which I lost interest in, grew out of or refused to wear, more often than not ended up on Rachel Jones from across the road. I enjoyed seeing Rachel in my clothes. I thought of it as some sort of bonding process which brought us closer as friends. I often remarked upon a dress or a trouser-suit which looked better on her. I never realised that my words probably did more harm than help. Naturally, I thought my mother and I were being generous, but Rachel's family must have wondered how we could squander such possessions when we lived on the poor side. A pair of shoes were raked from somewhere, from where exactly I never knew, because I don't remember them ever being mine. All I knew was that they were great, black, lumpy things which Rachel wouldn't like either.

Nevertheless, I was dragged to Rachel's house with the shoes, to be made guilty for being an ungrateful child.

The following morning I was neither shocked nor stunned when Rachel burst into tears of embarrassment at the ugly pair of shoes on her feet. She didn't want to go to school. We knew where the Comprehensive boys hid and where we could, but I'll never know why I decided not to go to school that morning. I pitied Rachel and knew that I would be wearing those shoes if I weren't so ungrateful. Forgetting who initially had the idea, we hid inside the arch (a tunnel the river ran through), until mid-morning. Fear or hunger (or a combination of both) prised us out to find two sets of parents searching the river.

After 1985 some parts of the Rhondda Valleys hit unemployment rates over sixty-five per cent, and everywhere in Wales employment was its lowest for over half a century. Although the disappearance of all working pits would soon be final, the actual closure of the coal mines was hardly an issue anymore: most had been closed for ages; the rise, or not, of government unemployment benefits was more the norm in conversation. Only one major mine remained open. Luckily my Dad, the professional miner, worked there. Mammy had an afternoon and sometimes evening bar job at the pub at the top of the road. Later she would clean Treorchy Library and I would begin to read books by the hour. Income was healthy. Each aspect of our family life was healthy and happy. A Mam, a Dad, a big brother, two cats, a dog and a goldfish.

The unexpected income enabled my parents to mortgage a house further up the village, making our stay at Lower Terrace rather brief.

It was in the midst of winter when I first visited our soon-to-be new house. We sat on crates in the parlour with an oil lamp burning. My mother smoked but my breath was visible too. The house smelt damp, a smell, strangely enough, I particularly favour, but this smell was different. It smelt not only damp but dirty. The foul smell lingered around the house as if the walls were made of wet sheets. I'd never been inside an empty house before, every one in Wales could have smelt worse, but something was definitely not right.

The previous owners (after becoming divorcees) left nothing more than a 1960s leather settee and a few summer catalogues. We walked on concrete and the wallpaper, ripped back, revealed partly broken, blackened plaster. It was a large house with an air of disability. There was no supernatural presence, just a pattern to the veins of the walls and a chill which seemed destined to last longer than the snowfall.

Nevertheless, our brown carpets, brown curtains, the coffee table James had made in school, Mammy's yellow bed clothes, my three-storey Barbie house and all our other furniture was relocated to serve us in my third home.

3

At the back of our house two sheds stood side by side. One was Dad's fishing shed, the other my play shed. Furnished with wooden wardrobes, drawers and desks, painted white, my shed was the largest, most windproof 'Wendy-house' in existence. My mother made pretty net curtains for the windows, and both Mam and Dad filled my cupboards with games, dolls and books. Books were my favourite; I fell in love with literature. If the opportunity arose to lag to work with my mother in the early evening, I snatched it. One of my most cherished childhood memories is being locked in Treorchy Public Library on my own. Of course my mother was dusting or vacuuming away in a corner but the building was so large the likelihood of us crossing paths was slim and only when she had called my name twenty times would I disappointedly return to the back door to leave with her. If she had threatened to leave me there, I would have been quite happy to sleep on the leather benches with Oliver Twist or Huckleberry Finn, except she never threatened, she insisted I leave. The library was, make no bones about it, my favourite place in the whole wide world.

Literature and little else appeared to interest me. Graham next door became an exception because I was sure he could have become a novel in his own right. I was told he was 'weird', this of course was a subject close to my own heart and I watched him carefully. He must have been fifty, maybe sixty years old, his body a matured cherub, with a big rounded belly and yellow stringy curls, turned grey. Sightings were most frequent in the garden where he'd appear at 6 o'clock each evening attending to his outside toilet. He wore sparkling white Y-fronts and a vest of excessive size and was always followed by Princess, his squealing corgi. He went to church, once on Wednesday and twice on Sunday, accompanied by his man friend George who collected him in a shiny red car. He spoke eloquently, and sometimes whilst reading in the kitchen I could hear him singing hymns gracefully in his outhouse. I often found myself with my face pushed against the glass of his front window; it was never any use: the view was always hidden with fresh flowers of all colours, shapes and sizes and a huge pink table-lamp. Dad said he was asking for a break-in, displaying such lavish items in his window, but I never understood why anyone should want to steal the flowers when they could just as easily go and pick some.

I remember once being invited in. I forget the occasion but I was with my mother, and to my amazement, I found myself in Graham's front porch. And quickly found it reasonable that he had once hired Michelangelo to decorate his hallway.

I never knew whether I was attracted to Graham because I wondered whether I was as strange as he, but once I had satisfied all my curiosity about the man, he wasn't strange any more. He was a harmless, happy, slight eccentric who sent me birthday cards signed 'Graham & Princess'. My last card came on my thirteenth, with 'You Are a Teenager at Last' or words to that effect printed on the front. I was always puzzled as to how he knew my forwarding address. Three months later his name appeared in the Obituaries column of the *Rhondda Leader*.

Outside my shed in a patch of earth, a cemetery had begun to appear. All the dead insects I found in the garden I put into jewellry boxes from H.Samuel which once housed gifts of earrings and chains for my mother. I named them and dug graves for them. I didn't so much look for dead butterflies as kill perfectly healthy ones and apologise by making wooden crosses to plant in the earth above them. I often dug them up again to check for any change or movement. The colourful spots of death neither moved nor changed and it sometimes disappointed me, although I came to expect no progress. From a very early age I found avid interest in death. I knew very little about the subject and the only incidents which came close to experience both involved pet goldfish. My first pet (excluding Bella who had been with me as far back as I could remember), was a fish named Flower. I found him one day in an ashtray, half hidden by my brother and his friends' ash. I studied a while before my mother stomped in shouting 'James, I told you to flush it.' My grief amounted to little more than confusion as I asked, 'Why isn't Flower working?' The second had been Flower's replacement, Jaws. He nearly died in Lower Terrace when my father mistakenly filled his bowl with water from the kettle. My mother appeared from around a corner, ran him under cold water, put his head in her mouth, squeezed her buttocks together, created a vacuum of air somewhere within her body and blew it into Jaws. He lived and when she told me she had given him the kiss of life, I began to think she could bring everything back to life with a magical gust of oxygen which only she possessed.

I found myself lured to burial places. My mother told me that my tomb was in Jerusalem, and it took me a long time to figure out that I had been named after Rebecca from the Bible, after temporarily thinking that my grave had already been dug. I was told my fascination was a morbid abnormality, which obviously added to my feeling of strangeness. I hadn't the vocabulary to understand that cemeteries are peaceful retirements for those passed on and gravestones a token of love. Always fascinated by words, I found headstone inscriptions all the more engaging. How do you sum up a person's life in two well-wishing sentences? How can one venerate a place one will inevitably occupy?

It surprised me how quickly circles of friends diminished and grew according to which direction you walked home from school. Rachel drifted away into a once-important, now forgotten individual and Louise, it seemed, had been waiting to befriend me since before I had been born. Louise's family confused me. Like everything else, they were different from my own. She had two younger sisters with funny names, and no brothers. My mother told me that it was every mother's dream to have girls and boys, but some women could only have girls. I automatically assumed that women with two children of the same sex could not fulfil their dream and I had formed an invisible bond of sympathy for Louise's mother long before I had met her. Louise's father, Robert, was a farmer or maybe a forestry labourer. (I remember him wearing wellies, green cords, a degrained Arran jumper, a waxcoat and a daicap, everywhere he went). Their house wasn't cluttered with things which her mother had collected over forty-two years, eighteen houses and two marriages like ours was. In fact it was bare apart from a television and a settee, more like a newly married childless couple's. Louise was expected to help clean, cook and wash dishes which I found particularly strange. They ate very little at mealtimes, so little you would think food was being rationed.

Everything was dealt with in orderly fashion. Mornings were worked around a rota. The children would go downstairs in their pyjamas and eat cereal with their mother. If they ate it all they could eat toast as well. Then wash, dress and brush teeth, school, out to play, bake a cake, vacuum the huge bare room, no watching television in the sun and no picking blackberries in the rain.

I was not only strange to the extent of being an alien faced with a human society, I was inferior as well. Louise's family was the first practical shock to the theory system. I was always well fed, well clothed and well housed, then left to unravel the mysteries of death, religion and Shakespeare on my own. No order, no clothes to peg out, drink Coca-Cola first thing in the morning, eat cheese last thing at night.

I never doubted that Louise's mother was a very good mother, but mine was better. Often whilst sitting on Louise's bed, Louise would take a packet of sanitary towels from her wardrobe and hmph, 'She always puts these in here, I don't need them,' and return them to her parents' bedroom. Who would just leave some

16

female hygiene stuff in their daughter's room, three years early without a word of explanation? I recall a certainty of 'my mother would never do that'.

Louise went to church with her sisters. To me it seemed like another point of order in their lives. A type of school at the weekend, so that they could go home, bake a cake and vacuum the huge bare room on their days off as well. I was often asked to go but the only religion I lived by was saying please and thank you when my Gran invited the Jehovah's Witnesses in for tea.

On Sundays I read, and it didn't take much reading to know that all important people went to church. Madonna was a Catholic. (My taste in literature had turned gradually to *Just Seventeen* and *Smash Hits*).

A few weeks later I was a member of the church choir. One pound for Sundays and two pound for weddings. It was a simple process of giving and taking but by any Christian terms I was cheating the church (offering my services because I wanted to be a pop-star), and the church were cheating themselves (buying services from little girls who wanted nothing to do with God, but appear in magazines in scanty halter-neck tops). There was no excitement in sitting in the freezing cold, on splintering wooden seats; still, someone thought I could sing! The closest I came to a spiritual feeling there was having an about-to-be married groom wink at me in the midst of a serious wedding service.

One day, someone left the back door wide open. Bella trotted out of the house to meet a handsome young Alsatian. She could see from his collar his name was Ben, he'd watched her from afar for some time, and seeing the door open today, couldn't pass on the chance to meet the beautiful bitch in full personal glory. He invited her to his penthouse kennel on the outskirts of California. Bella looked once, twice at my shed, wanting to say goodbye, but the opportunity being too overwhelming to wait for my return from Louise's or from Church, she quickly accompanied Ben in cantering out of the dry Hendrefadog street and onto the road to far, far away.

At midnight I had arrived home from the mountain with my mother to meet my brother and father at the house. Neither had sighted either Alsatian. Fingers were not directly pointed but I knew that whilst I was out of the room, the blame was balancing on my head. I spent the night curled up against the cooker on the hairs that Bella had left behind. I was cold and my mother said Bella would be as well. I conjured most events into fairy-tale stories in order to simplify the complications of life, but I was living realistically enough to know that a mention of California then could have killed me.

Nobody was to work, nobody was to attend school, church, have a meal or bath until that dog was found. And naturally, for the first week nobody did.

The phone calls, the posters, the advertisements and the long, day-lasting, health-risking searches were of no avail.

Gradually, coal mining, cleaning, panel beating and poetry began again, but with a tarpaulin of melancholy sheeting its every moment and face. Everything moved at a tortoise-like speed which I had never seen before.

After each phone call received I would wait at the door for my mother to return, exhaustedly shake her head and make her way to the kitchen for a cigarette. A word could have shaken the two-month silence which froze the entire house.

Bella was two years younger than I. I'd not known life without the dog, and if someone were to say 'I understand, she's like part of the family' ever again they were sure to be the victim of my lethal clenched fists. I came to understand indirect insults, only when I was the butt of them.

It only became appropriate to switch the television on another month later but reading a book would still have been ignorant. There is nothing like an irreplaceable loss to put a hold on everything you would like to do and indeed, a hold on everything you took and would like to take advantage of.

18

It was a Sunday and normal life had resumed. Dad was fishing and James at his girlfriend's. Mammy had been drying dishes until she heard the knock. As she dropped a towel and passed me on the way, I think I witnessed my mother's first half-smile for four whole months. Before she had been out of the room for five minutes and before I relocated to the shed Bella ran through the house with a healthy whine. Weighing my arms around her neck, I cried every tear I would have liked to in previous months.

An angel had known we had suffered enough and sent Bella back, telling Ben to go and show his fancy kennel to an unwanted mongrel.

4

I looked in the mirror and decided I was an ugly girl. My eyes droopy and oversized, my bones wrapped in thin blue sheeting which would need fifty-two weeks of sun merely to turn pink, my hair long, straggled and ginger and my entire face plastered with blemishes and freckles. Looking at Louise, and comparing our appearance rain or shine, I came out the faultier.

Ten years of my mother's 'It's not ginger, it's a lovely golden mousey', didn't compare to three years of classroom 'It's not golden, it's ginger'.

'Freckles are a sign of beauty' to plain and simple, 'Freckle-face' and 'You're slim like your mother' to 'Rebecca Skinny milinx'.

True, my mother was slim and still beautiful, with a head of ash-blonde hair. (I never knew she dyed until I began to dabble in the wonders of beauty chemistry four years later). She had what was called a 'Powell' nose, a small, straight affair which sat neatly in the middle of her pink face. Every aspect of my mother was perfect apart from a collection of thread veins she kept inside each cheek. If I looked too long or too hard at this disappointing feature, I summoned myself to sharply look away, so as not to spoil the flawless image of her I carried, and selfishly not to remind myself that this was what I had coming, to add to my already jigsaw-looking ginger and white face.

Where did the ginger come from? That's what I wanted to know. Couldn't ask Mam, she'd say, 'Golden, not ginger.' I asked my brother if my father was ginger although I didn't think he was, because James wasn't. He said, 'A ginger moustache.' So maybe I wasn't adopted, but I wasn't pretty either.

I had once known that the best girls in the world weren't pretty, but in an ever-moving bubbly pop-music world Jane Eyre and George Eliot's 'Maggie' couldn't compare with Janet Jackson and Kylie Minogue. I was ugly and nobody or nothing could change it.

And then Dad was made redundant. I took the day off school to go out with my mother and father. We went to the Lion Hotel in Treorchy and sat under a picture which housed the slogan 'On Thin Ice'. It was Dad's favourite saying if I were insolent. 'You're on thin ice, girl.' I understood it but had a tendency to pretend I didn't. I believed that if I laughed in the face of seriousness it wouldn't be serious any more. My mother and I ate ham, Dad had steak. I drank Coca-Cola afterwards and Mammy sipped on vodka. I didn't quite understand why we were celebrating people losing jobs from the last pit in South Wales. 'Not celebrating,' Dad said, 'just making the most of it.' The wads of money we had felt that morning with widened eyes and then thrown around the kitchen was why we were celebrating. Dad said it was his ticket to a life of leisure. He said he would be able to go to Mumbles pier with his fishing rod, every single day. But it didn't quite work out like that.

Instead of fishing, my father began to follow my mother to work. In the mornings ancient pieces of rock and mineral which sat in the reference library filtered their way into Dad's pockets and ended up on my dressing table. I declined walking home from school to an empty house and instead joined my family in the Dare Hotel. My mother behind the bar and my father at the other side, I played pool, drank Coca-Cola and ate cheese and onion crisps while others would have been waiting for chips to be cooked and watching *Neighbours*. Within two months I was pool champion of the pub. I amused a male adult audience with stories and chalk cartoons on the dart blackboard. I had the entire unemployed or layabout community of Hendrefadog to

21

help me with my homework. Tea times turned into evenings and evenings turned to nights. My mother proceeded to the other side of the bar to spend her earnings.

Gradually, things changed. What began as a harmless collection of anecdotes and a trivial matter of absorbing wanted attention became simply much more sinister. It would have been my father's birthday when I realised that everything was duller than I was perceiving it to be. The taxi that we desperately needed arrived, but Dad refused to get in.

'I'm not getting in there, where are you taking me? I'm not going.'

'We're taking you home, for Christ's sake.'

He staggered around the yard as though he were carrying thirty stone on his back, before falling against the wall. He slouched down, ready to sleep. Three men emerged from the pub and lifted him into the car, and then into the house. Three hours later he was outside holding onto the railings of the chapel crying, 'Let me out, let me out.' My mother was at the window throwing fishing trophies, one by one to the floor. Although at first I laughed at his drunken antics and only became slightly distressed when they went on too long; it seemed as though it was destined to happen. I may never have been sure until this point that both my parents were alcoholics, but there must have been a few unmemorable sign-posts to their destination, because disgusting as all the snoring on the settee was and as horrible as the smell of vodka percolating through the downstairs was, it seemed like the most natural thing in the world.

In a desperate attempt to deny myself knowledge of something I knew quite a lot about, I picked up my skateboard and skated far far away from the house and the pub and stumbled upon a place called Railway Terrace. Because Railway Terrace was a secluded street separated from the rest of Hendrefadog on one side by stables and on the other by a steep, zig-zag road, the kids didn't bother to find friends their own age and all played together.

22

Rounders on the junction which was seldom used, swimming in the dam on the higher side of the arch and cycling down the old railway line. In the evenings they sat on top of the garages throwing stones into the air and watching the slow-moving world go by. Icky and I always stayed the longest which in my case was safest and when I was sure it couldn't get any darker I jumped into the stingies, picked up my skateboard and took the longest route home. Icky's mother was probably an alcoholic. His brothers ran a stolen car racket and swore a lot. Gemma and Lisa's father had died a year before; and Tilly had a whole collection of blood-stained knickers on her roof. Generally speaking, they were my kind of people. I hadn't long been a member of the self-styled Railway Gang before we began to find fun in 'Knock the door, Ginger'. Reg in Barrett Street always gave good chase, and good chase is everything in the game. It was only because we had exhausted all the fun in each other that we decided to aggravate other people. What he didn't realise was, every time he picked up his walking stick and struggled after us down the street shouting 'You little bastards, I'll kill you', with his stupid Jack Russell behind him, he was making a large contribution to childish joy. When his legs got too bad and he just opened the door to shout 'I'll set fire to your Bonfire wood, tonight' (which we thought was just plain nasty), we couldn't be bothered any more either.

Bonfire night was approaching and we had been collecting all autumn: wood and newspaper, tables and chairs, crates and anything else burnable; and stored it in a garage. When the day came, a Wednesday, we all took the day off school to prepare. All the mothers had made food. I had tried to have little contact with my parents, but I thought that if I just asked them to make some burgers and show up sober everything would be okay, just for that day. And stressed how important it all was to me. How important it would be for the Railway Gang to see me with my perfect mother and father. How important it would have been for them to realise that I wasn't the unhappy stray they always knew I was.

So, I waited patiently in a circle around our mega fire with the other children and their parents. We lit one or two fireworks and ate some burned toast, and then my brother's car came around the corner. Tears began to hit my shoes before I got to the car, and when I did it just got worse. He and Cathy lifted out two bags of beefburgers and James said, 'She's gone down the Dare, she'll see you later.'

Ultimately, I would have loved to turn around and run straight into the fire. I had been preparing not just a bonfire but a Railway Children shock. Their shock would make this bonfire night the best day of my life; like everything else, it hadn't quite worked out. The children stood curious and interested, waiting. I could see 'I told you so' on their lips and didn't want them to look at me any longer. I ran and ran. But where could I run to?

I was woken one night by screaming. I went to investigate and as though it was exactly what I expected, I saw my father beating my mother's head against the telephone stand. Devoid of thoughts, I dived downstairs and landed on my father's back. Painfully thin, I made no impact and fell off. I'd left my bed knowing exactly what was happening, just as it'd been happening for months and I'd told myself subconsciously that I would ignore it once again. I thought I hated both of my parents. Bella looked up at me, too stupid to help. Behind her was a mound of dirty dishes and one gleaming saucepan on the draining board. As I'd probably seen in a strange silent movie, I ran and smashed it against Dad's red face and again across the back of his head.

I spent the night in my mother's blue Avenger, parked at the back of the Chinese in Parc Road. For an hour or two my mother and I listened to the argument alive and kicking in the closed shop. We listened, and laughed at the velocity and the high pitch the owner made of her peculiar language; my mother smoked a few cigarettes and I went to sleep.

It was three or four in the morning when we were both woken abruptly by two policemen.

'What are you doing here at this time, love?'

'What's it got to do with you?'

'A lot when we see a child of this age sleeping in a car.'

'I'm hiding from my husband.'

'Why?

'Because he's horrible,' I chirped in.

They lost interest and told us to be careful, before leaving.

Dad was becoming the enemy my father had once been. The bruises, the tears and the nights in the car were exactly the same but I wasn't. This time I was seven years older and I had the discomfort of understanding it all. I had a first-class seat for the showing of a dysfunctional marriage. I saw my mother with another man. I saw my father drink until he couldn't keep it down. I saw the broken plates and the warm blood stain the carpet and heard my mother's head beat against the wall, time after time. Dull thumping over and over as she blacked out to the thrum tee thrum, thrum tee thrum of her head. My heart thrum tee thrummed with a black beating of anger which I had no means of expressing or using.

I was old enough to know exactly what was wrong and the depth of damage that was being caused, but I was too young to know what to say or what to do. I didn't know because I didn't know what I wanted. I thought about Mam moving in with her boyfriend and I thought about another divorce. I thought about putting up with it and I thought about telling my grandparents but all the things I could possibly think about led to more violence, more heartbreak and more of what I had been silencing all my life.

So mostly I lived in my shed and I avoided both parents more than they avoided each other. Hunched in a corner, I felt like a monkey walking on egg shells. Hear no, see no, speak no evil.

5

It was a September evening in 1987, a week after I had started Comprehensive school, when I was lying in bed with the lights out, attempting to sleep. My door creaked open. He stood hairy and intoxicated in white boxer shorts. He moved closer to my bed. I turned away and declined to keep open my eyes.

The smell of stale cider filled my room.

The blankets were pulled back and the mattress rustled as he got into bed and embraced my fragile eleven-year-old body. I could feel his fleshy bulk at hair's-breadth, slowly moving towards, touching my skin. I screwed up my face with stubbornness and hoped that if I lay perfectly still, he might leave. Besides, fear had rooted me to the sheets because somehow I had an idea of what would happen next.

He reached out his fat hand as I curled up senselessly, momentarily believing I could protect myself. He gripped my white cotton 'Tuesday' knickers and held my arms tightly, bruising them immediately as he did so. There was a lot of fumbling and dull pain, and five minutes into the skirmish the dull transformed to the extreme.

He broke my hymen and my senses alike.

After ten minutes he stood up, lifted his shorts and nervously staggered to the open door, 'If-you-tell-your-mother-she-will-get-the-beating-of-her-life-and-so-will-you.' He strung his words together with no pauses and left me in a puddle of blood and bodily fluid. Tears which I hadn't noticed until then streamed down my face and landed on my thirsty tongue.

I stared at my knickers between my legs. White cotton soaked in bright oxygenated blood. The 'Tuesday' and the pretty little yellow flowers barely visible. Too dumbfounded to move or think, I heard the return of my mother, the rain incessant on the window and the walls of the house close down to night. Each minute passed like a lifetime.

At daylight I folded the blood-stained, once-lemon sheets and red-drenched panties into a clumsy ball and crept downstairs. Every move was like a real life touch the metal and the buzzer goes off game. I found a sufficient hiding place in my shed. There I stuffed the linen into a chunky wooden drawer occupied by 'Connect 4' and three scantily clad Barbie dolls.

I began to scrub my skin until it bled. An eleven-year-old red, patchy burning body in a bath of disinfectant. It took around a month before I knew the sticky dirtiness would remain forever.

There was no life after rape. Trust and the word 'trust' jumped out of my vocabulary and exploded in a suffocating lack of air, landed in a gathering of rose petals before my feet.

I acquired two phobias that evening: the fear of open doors and a fear of people. All people.

Life seemed to be a process of ripping children out of themselves. I chose to exclude myself from this practice. Somehow I ended up in a glass coffin. A dwelling where I could see and hear life going on around me, but where participating would not be possible.

Speaking was not possible. I could relive the rape every night and console myself by hiding at the bottom of my bed, but to say a word as simple as 'yes' became a hindering task which provoked tears and aroused suspicion.

My mother decided I should go to the doctor's; she told him I was extremely withdrawn and that I cried all the time. He sat in front of me and spoke an inaudible blend of English and Pakistani. The colour of his skin clashed with his white surgery. If his English had been perfect I would have refused even more so to listen to his endless questions and suggestions. 'I'll prescribe for you a tonic.' Did that translate to 'I'll give you cyanide which will end your suffering'? Nobody could be trusted, so I hoped it did.

Nobody knew of the incident. If they had they would have realised that my inability to speak and listen was caused simply by the physical effects of rape. It was true that my physical state deteriorated; for weeks I felt as though a broomstick had been wrenched between my legs, thrust through my body and the brush stuck in my throat. There was a lot of blood and a lot of vomit. I was constantly worried that my legs were falling out of my hips. My skin began to flake due to constant scraping and scrubbing.

The reason I chose not to speak or to listen was simply because people could not be trusted, and what they had to say was probably lies. I had not become a sudden victim to madness. I had become a sudden victim to a bastard. And I have never looked at another human being with as much affection and lack of suspicion since.

As much as I searched for sufficient reasons in order to make the incident as normal as possible, there was no explanation for someone to turn around and rape me. Faced with this type of situation a child is only capable of creating a wall of paranoia. The world was against me.

The post-rape threat didn't live up to be any kind of threat. My mother had already, four times in total, got the beating of her life, and it seemed inevitable that she would get another if I spoke or not. After living a week with a bleeding uterus and a broomstick wedged inside my gut, getting beaten would have been of minimal discomfort. Threat? I could have laughed at this statement if it didn't remind me so much of his naked blood-stained body. I couldn't tell anyone simply because my mother would kill him, go to jail and I would be orphaned. Or perhaps she wouldn't believe me and put me in care. People would know. People would mock me. People would know that I was not normal. I didn't particularly care about anything. I lived in a see-through box, the inside looking out. Nothing really mattered.

My life up until this point had been that of a child's. An affair of balance. Happenings consisted of black and white, wrong and right. Suddenly I was shadowed with various shades of grey, and it is this I associate with the loss of innocence, the first decision I alone had to make. The wall of confusion which is supposed only to hinder adults gave me a barrier to cower behind. The loss of virginity, I tried to fool myself, had nothing to do with it and happened later in life. Of course I knew really that both aspects of innocence were unduly stolen from me.

6

So compelling is my notion that falling asleep facing upward will cause my death, I believe it could work in reverse. They're going to bury me on my side.

When I was eleven years old and I desperately wanted to die I began to deny my lungs oxygen. I closed my mouth, my eyes and my mind and I lay still with my arms crossed on my chest. My routine daily failed so miserably, that I discovered it was impossible to kill yourself in such a pathetic manner. I also discovered it is impossible for me to sleep on my back. I assured myself that if I managed it I would most definitely die. And I tried to draw my last breath, to sleep with my head to the sky.

It was probably early evening. The big yellow bomb was sinking. The cheerful light bounced off the stainless-steel pole in the garden. I could see it from where I was standing on the bed. My father hung off the edge of the bed hiding his face while my mother screamed and kept on screaming, 'My carpet, my bloody carpet.' I never liked the lamp anyway. The pattern was rather like fingerprints; fingerprints made me sick. The mess we called painting in infants' school where we dipped our hands in paint and then slapped them on paper, I always hated that. The grooves did it, so human and unique like the hairs beginning to appear under my arms, sickening.

I don't remember what happened. I only saw the end, the violent climax. The lamp was heavy and it cracked either side of my father's head. The atmosphere, like a roaring drunk, split, and numbed into a dull hangover. There were phone calls and screaming and ambulances and in the middle of it my father disappeared. He ran, holding his head up like a mother holding a baby's, out into the streets. I kept watching the pole all through. The sun beating on it, and blood pumping from his head and my mother screaming like a background to it all, and I'm beating, a throbbing numbness taking all words, actions and feelings away. But I couldn't stop staring at the pole. The magnolia paint peeling, the sun and the shadow. The police took fifteen minutes to arrive and left five minutes later. They looked at the lamp fragments and the bloody carpet and said 'Well, it is quite heavy, but a domestic, luv, we can't do much if you don't know where he is.'

She said, 'I think he'll need stitches.'

They said, 'Well, let's hope the ambulance finds him.'

Let's hope the ambulance doesn't find him. Let's hope he bleeds to death. The numbing opened a little in my head, just enough to be able to think up a few words. I didn't murmur, of course. I just kept watching that pole.

It made my problems different from any other child's violent upbringing. It made my father and my mother almost as bad as one another; my mother never cried for help or tried to run away.

She didn't live in fear, afraid to move: she always gave as good as she got. Sometimes it was almost as though my mother and father were a drinking, fighting Romeo and Juliet. Was it meant to be like that? I hurt and I cried and the sight of black and blue frightened me, but I was never sure if I was just being too sensitive, because it seemed so much like they enjoyed arguing for argument's sake.

The season of goodwill crept up on my family unnoticed. Life went on around me unnoticed. It was only when my mother asked me if we should bother trimming up that I remembered Christmas was around the corner. And even then it wasn't anything to worry about. Mammy would work, Dad would get rat-arsed and I would go on. Invisible.

I focused on the amber streetlight when I felt the broomstick for a sixth time. He got rat-arsed and forgot to close curtains. My inside was numb as well now. Hollowed out so that anyone or anything felt free to intrude. Rubbing against, wearing out and dirtying my heart, my lungs, my liver and everything which once belonged to me. There was nothing to hurt and everything to claim so he may as well just crush me like a big brown slug and breathe loudly and irregularly through his sweaty nose like he was. I don't know who loosened first when there was knocking at the front door. Louise. She had invited me to Midnight Mass. The minute Jesus Christ was born, thousands and thousands of years later, I was getting raped.

So, it began to hurt my hollowness when I thought about my father-father. I couldn't remember enough about him, only that he had a ginger moustache, and I couldn't forget enough about my step-father because I knew I knew too much. There was no yes and no and there was no in between. I forgot what a father was in one day when it had taken me five years to learn.

It was after New Year when my mother accidentally stopped it all. She did something outrageous and she did it for herself. The love I harboured for what she was doing never connected with the hate I felt for her doing it. She had been pushed, squeezed to the brink but that didn't change the fact that this could be a clear end to a very energy-consuming battle. I avoided high water and lived through hell to stop her doing it and that squeezed me into a place far beyond the edge.

She stepped away and he fell flat on his back. I couldn't see the knife. My mother kept backing towards me. Creeping gently, shaking, the back of her head getting closer to my face. When she was gone the realisation was overwhelming. It was much too much to think about and I stepped toward my father with a phrase I thought would orphan me: 'Curiosity killed the cat', but when I got there, when I finally saw that she had missed it was as dull as it was when she first opened the kitchen drawer.

Orphanage couldn't be so bad. Could not be as horrible as the breadknife planted through the inside of his upper arm. Over and over again, I kept seeing my step-father's bloody arm.

For a while the house was silent. I knew all about silence and wasn't surprised to learn that violence could quieten you down. Neither my mother nor my father knew or cared about it one way or the other. They were too busy rationing words to fight each other. So it was me who had to step off the edge of the world because if I didn't, we all would.

Love, hate and confusion were circling the place like central heating. They played the love/hate games and I sat staring, contemplating but never solving the wall of confusion.

It was summer again when I decided I'd had enough. Sunday afternoon my mother and my step-father drank too much at lunch-time to continue persevering with the dinner and they both went to bed. It wasn't often they did go to bed together. Dad slept in the front room or Mam slept with me. Sometimes she never came home and Dad slept with me. Now and again Mam would sit up all night or she'd clean the kitchen or sit in the car. Dad still worried about 'our secret' and would only pop in then. Pop in.

And it didn't sound much like they were in bed. Thumping and shouting and chaos which made me numb again. She was the first downstairs. 'He says he's going to kill himself. I'm going to help him.' The rattling of pills and glass my mother was producing caused a pain in my stomach. The pain in my stomach I knew I could lose if I helped her to help myself. Before I heard a word my mother said, I was delivering pints of water and rainbows of prescription killers to my father's bedside. When everything was there she held his head and threw some pills in while I tilted water into his filthy mouth. So absolute was my wish to kill him by then, it felt right. 'I'm cleansing the dirtiness that resides in my house and life.' I thought his punishment was so soft, winding up in tranquillity while his crime was so slow, ongoing and incurable.

'Die,' we chanted while the easy-way-outs found their places. 'Die you bastard,' my mother said in the doorway. 'Die, die, die,' I screamed while I stamped around the bed, looking into the eyes of the monster I had been afraid to look at for so long.

They were closing slightly, but not enough. 'Die.' I dived on the dying thing with a pillow and held it over his face. 'Die,' said the eleven-year-old who was already emotionally dead. And all the time my mother thought I was doing it for her sake. 'Die,' she said softly, as she dragged me out and closed the door.

We sat for four hours eating Turkish Delight and smiling silently before one of us had to say it. Anxious and still hungry, I asked meekly, 'Shall I check?' I don't remember if my father was lying, snoring like a fat king of animals in the bed, or if my mind has been contaminated by old *Brookside* episodes and he was loitering in the doorway, still alive and ugly as ever. I do remember my mother behind me sighing, 'Naw, naw, naw, he's been sick.'

No. No. No.

Again the house was funeral-quiet. Yet nobody had died, at least not clinically. Somewhere, ghosts were screaming, beings who had no means of making themselves clear or solidified. Spirits who were just crying for a door to open. Dying for an entrance into the audible world, but they were so far away, the glass was so air-tight. Nobody could hear a murmur.

Perhaps my brother heard the vibrations of my fists against the glass or the tap, tap, tap of my nails against the lid. The lid that would not open and the tap, tap, tapping that had slowed down to a non-existent speed because suffocation took away all energy. I'd see him once or twice a day sitting at the kitchen table. He resented our troubles because he'd rather be spraying a car or kissing his girlfriend. He was agitated and waiting for something to happen. Weren't we all?

It took four months for my mother to secretly remove all mortgage funds from the building society and pack them every Thursday into the boot of her car. Four months of phone calls to Social Security offices, housing estates and refuges. To hide the letters from the bank which would tell my father the house would be repossessed. To visit the council house she and I would adorn on the worst estate in South Wales. To pack essentials without anyone realising they had gone. And when the secretarial work had been finalised, what she called 'freedom' prevailed.

My mother made the speech that would make my father mad, in the company of my brother, and he put his arms around us to escort us to the door. His girlfriend put the last of our bags in the car. It was of comfort to see him helpless. Holding onto the fence so that he didn't fall down. I looked away, holding tears of some emotion back and turned to follow my mother.

A pain struck my neck and the more I tried to push the lid away, the more my weakness pulled me back. My step-father held my hair so tightly I believed my neck was breaking. And I'd rather it break than be pulled back in. I stumbled away, and hanging onto the ledge of the step I saw his hand with my hair inside it. My mother snatched at me, and James's girlfriend closed the door on my brother holding my step-father's throat.

Words and hurt is all I could feel. 'Freedom. This. Going. Get. Safe.' Everything is hurting me. 'Only way.' 'Safe.'

No, I have not escaped.

7

My father-father never had a fixed occupation. He worked in Port Talbot steelworks for a long time and he worked in various factories for a short time, but in 1964 he was building a housing estate on top of a mountain. And he was paid well because he wasn't just building, he was keeping a secret for the local council. While attempting to level ground the labourers kept finding skeletons. Thousands of human skeletons. The rumour filtering in the men's homes was that they were building on a Roman burial ground.

Twenty years before my father stepped foot on the mountain, my Grandfather Powell drove past it every morning on his way to work and swore blind he spoke to a beheaded man called Rhys there. Obviously people had their suspicions, but once my father had been given his last pay-off, the estate was, for reasons unknown, named Penrhys.

My mother and I moved into a house on the outskirts of the estate shortly before Christmas 1991, by which time it was the drug and crime capital of the Valleys; and the most mentioned location on the subject of poverty and trouble anywhere in Wales. Surrounded by forest and a two-mile stretch from civilisation, the police avoided Penrhys because it made their lives safe and generally less stressful. It was prison for the innocent and a haven for the criminal, a situation which would continue to plague my life, but only partly because I lived on the estate.

An institution of lowlifeitus forced me to lock myself in my bedroom with a few hundred books and my brother's old Clash records. And so life remained silent. I hardly saw, let alone spoke to my mother, but somewhere around that time I started smoking her cigarettes. Smoking and reading and listening to shattering glass. Listening to *London Calling* and watching the closed door with anxiousness and watching through the window the sky turn red at night, and sleeping curled like a cat at the bottom of my bed in the early hours of the morning. Watching, and waiting for normality to come. Compelled to walk where I could find peace of mind, where I could be safe. Around and around the bedroom in circles, circles, circles, too scared to go out but too scared to stay in, and all hours of the day I heard smashing in the distance. Why wouldn't someone shatter my glass?

Soon after I had completed George Orwell's *Nineteen Eighty Four*, the man who lived next door but one was kicked to death in his garden. I convinced myself later that I heard his screaming over the Sex Pistols' *Who Killed Bambi?* But in actual fact I was lucky enough to have only seen and climbed over the police cordons on my way to school, early the following morning. What looked like a circus-type tent had been erected on our pathway and while people crowded around it for a glimpse of blood, I kept on walking, thinking I knew enough dead souls already.

Years later I remember watching the Prince of Wales on a boyfriend's television being questioned about the problem areas of South Wales. 'Yeeeas,' he said, 'Aye have bin toold a lot about an estate oan a mountain called Penrhys, which we are raising funds foar.'

And while I gritted my teeth the whole magical world of Royalty fell to its knees in a hypocritical embarrassment. Who could want to be the mating machine of a corrupt, power-driven, lazy-arse family like that, anyway? Suddenly the word 'whore' sounded sweeter than 'princess'.

While sleeping on the kitchen floor next to Bella one evening I woke to her squealing and rolling on her back; pawing my shoulder as though asking me to call for an ambulance. When my mother arrived home in the morning I told her Bella had a large lump on her stomach. She looked at it and made phone calls.

Over a period of a month Bella had her cancer cut out and body stitched up, bit away her stitches and had more, bit away her stitches and got a cone collar which prevented her from doing anything but looking forward. She walked into tables, fell against door frames and became as miserable as I. Bella was locked in plastic which was supposed to make her better. We were both clawing at encasements hoping that there was some truth in the phrase 'Anything which doesn't kill you will make you stronger'.

I was under strict instructions not to take Bella's collar off but when my mother left for her boyfriend's house every night, I took it off. At nine I took her to a field and ran in circles, circles, circles with her. I cried, returning at eleven. My best friend and I could not talk, we were both in pain, we were both thirteen and living in giro land alone at midnight, but we found short interludes of pleasure in running and we escaped, three hours a day.

But still I was going crazy and still Bella kept on squealing. One day my auntie knocked on the door and took Bella to her car. I watched from the window, Bella walking, dying ungracefully with a plastic lampshade still attached to her head. I felt devastation take me by the wrist and shake me so violently my mother couldn't get close enough to wipe the tears away.

I hated my mother because she wasn't close, yet I wouldn't let her get any closer. I didn't notice if she tried. Her boyfriend's name was Martin and he lived back down in Hendrefadog. He picked her up in the early evening and he lent her his car to get home in the morning. She complained when she was at home about my silence and my locking myself away. Understandably she was completely dogmatic about my so-called 'unfounded misery and lethargy'. It is impossible to remember a spoken word in Penrhys after Bella was put to sleep; however, screams and shouts are distastefully familiar. My mother's genetic make-up seemed simple. Two halves of one person, the first being pure lady. Walking and talking and looking like the it-girl. She laughed, smiled and spoke like an angel; and the glamour of her presence was particularly relevant when I was small because children define people on sight, which could very well explain why we are such a looks-conscious population. And why only very sensible or very ugly people actually believe it is the inside that counts.

The less I spoke and the more I read and thought, the more difficult it became to see my mother in the same light. Too much had happened before my eyes. My mother only once attended a school parents' evening at Hendrefadog Primary. She was drunk and stole a cheese plant from the corridor. The images of her sinking vodka, holding knives, getting in Martin's car each evening were more memorable, more visual, more vivid. One proud motherly smile for each fifty 'I should have listened to the Doctor', to every thirty-five 'Go and live with your father'. There was no lady any more.

She had a face which turned me to stone many a time and eventually each insensitive word that left her throat sickened me, sickened me to the point where non-communication was an essential procedure, where before it was just a huge problem.

My periods began in the long, long silence that followed a horrendous battle. For two days I avoided telling her of her daughter's growth. It was something which didn't seem much like growing to me, because I already felt like an old woman who'd seen enough and was just waiting for death because it was the only thing left to see. Yet I knew vaguely that periods were supposed to be some kind of mother/daughter experience and in the middle of lifting a margarine tub from the fridge I stopped, stormed into the room where she was smoking after waking and said, 'I'm bleeding.'

'What?'

'I've been bleeding down there.'

'Why didn't you tell me?' she said.

She left as usual at seven that evening.

I smoked and read and bled and prayed and curled up like a cat at the bottom of the bed in the early hours of the morning.

Alone.

8

I soon realised that normality would not come. That the violation
could not be undone. I realized that however many miles away I
travelled from the rape scene, in an attempt to renew my memory,
the past binds the present. Physically, I was healed, and the
change of wallpaper suggested I had survived. But that was all I
had done. Made it out alive, but the power of the moment still
controlled me. A man who hangs himself from a tree without
breaking his neck, who is cut down by a paramedic in the vital
last seconds, lives on clinically, but mentally he is dead. The
bitter taste of mortality is stronger than the calcium which keeps
us whole, and will plague us forever. Knowing this I cared for
myself less than anything else.

I was caught with a group of people (whose names escape me, if
I ever knew them), on Dinas estate by the police. We had stolen
some clothes from somebody's washing line, or at least somebody
had, because I don't remember any clothes. Perhaps we just
intended it. They asked me my address, my age and they took
me home. I didn't tell them that nobody was in because they
didn't ask. They took me to Ton Pentre police station where I
waited for someone to take me to a faraway children's home. She
asked me in the car, the social worker, how old I was.

'I'm thirteen.'

'Well, I've left my children on their own, but never all night,
when they were thirteen.... What do you want to do, Rebecca?'

'About what?'

'I mean for a living.'

'I want to be a tattooist.'

'That's a strange occupation.'

Stupid cow. 'So people tell me.'

The home was only minimally scary because it looked quite like my school, except the blocks were named after colours instead of numbers. I was given a bed and a breakfast and then a man came to take me home again. 'Look upon this as an adventure,' the social worker said, 'but if it happens again you could be staying.'

When I got home my mother stood on the doorstep narrow-eyed and gap-toothed. I waited for the male social worker who had a twisted leg and couldn't walk fast enough and we went inside for another slanging match.

'You can't leave a child of this age in a house in Penrhys while you go off with your boyfriend, Mrs Williams.'

'You would if she was your daughter.'

'If you continue to do this you will be prosecuted and Rebecca will stay indefinitely.'

'Well take her.'

'You don't understand, our home is not somewhere you dump your children when you're bored with them.'

'Well, she's uncontrollable.'

'Perhaps she would be more controllable if she had a stable parent.'

I stayed in Martin's spare bedroom that evening and listened to some Queen cassettes while my mother and Martin went for a meal in West Wales. I hate Queen.

Apart from a few insincere greetings, my fourteenth birthday arrived and departed without excitement. Martin and my mother caught a flight to Corfu soon after. I was given Martin's house-keys to hold, simply because he wanted me to feed his cat, and so I travelled between Hendrefadog and Penrhys for two weeks. I experienced consenting sex for the first time in their bed with a man I knew briefly from Penrhys. It felt so wrong, so ungratifying, so sickening to the point of unconsciousness. Yet I continued to

41

sleep with the most unimaginative, undesirable person I have ever had the displeasure of meeting. Knowing, somewhere in a cavity of my mind, someone would eventually notice. My brother noticed the following day. I left my diary on the dining table, oblivious to the fact that he had a key too. He came seething in the night. He didn't want to meet Jonesy because he said he'd rip his face off. James said he wouldn't tell my mother if I stopped it there and then.

I had sex with Jonesy again and then spent the rest of the fortnight sick to the hilt.

My mother discovered my diary and disappointing behaviour in September 1992. She hit me three times around my head with her cluster of rings. Why, for one minute did I believe she'd put her arms around me and say 'Why didn't you tell me?' Instead I had the 'I didn't lose my virginity until I was nineteen' for the first time. And the first time was also the most vicious. Following two weeks of nine-to-five skirmish and six-to-eight consideration I asked Jonesy to round up some cash and catch a bus with me. And he did.

We spent our first night on the floor against a heater inside a ladies' toilet at a deserted bus-station just outside Birmingham. A lighted advertisement board kept me awake, cold, alone, even with company, anxious yet angry enough to find a strange uncomfortable place more sympathetic than my own home. I thought about how I got there. How striving for attention and healthy conversation can become so severe, what you end up with is much louder than what you wanted in the first place. How two wrongs can unintentionally break down the walls of Jericho. How such a furious din can become boring to the point of pushing you onto a bus to Cardiff and a hitch to beyond. I had become so confused, I didn't remember whether I wanted to speak or to hear. I just wanted to be free from air-tight walls, but what actually happened was the opposite. The walls got tighter.

We spent time in a Salvation Army hostel where all we had to do for a bed and a meal a day was admit we were Christians. We had a sing-song each night with people who were Scottish, were Irish, were English, but nobody showed the traits of being particularly religious. Jonesy could cash two giros away from home so the following Thursday we had enough to get a couple of bus tickets to somewhere else. Sort of like sticking a pin in a map when you can see a little through your blindfold, we stood at the bus watching the destinations and prices on the board flip over and over until I said, 'Yes, that one.'

We were woken by a gang of youths running past with pieces of computer equipment. It was early morning in a doorway on a boulevard whose name has faded into the years. Hungry, we walked, witnessing a prostitute being beaten with a baseball bat by a man with a BMW in Radford, Nottinghamshire's most notorious red light district. We stumbled at 4 am upon a café called Britannia. Open for twenty-four hours and guarded by Gus, a compulsive liar who I tried desperately to get closer to in the months I spent in his flat. He served us massive breakfasts, took us home and let me sleep in his bed. Introduced to the best pubs and clubs by a man who burnt his blue dreadlocks off while cooking and wore a bandana to hide the damage, I was lulled into a security that was dangerous, and yet it was 'Freedom. This. Going. Get', more solidified than the version my mother offered.

Camilla was a twenty-four-year-old Swedish girl with buck-teeth and a head of red and purple hair. She asked me to speak just to listen to my voice, reckoning the Welsh accent sounded similar to the Danish one and reminded her of her Scandinavian home. She occasionally slept on Gus's floor and was looking for a man to marry in order to stay in Britain legally, and I earnestly hoped she'd choose Jonesy.

Sam Glam lived downstairs and wore pink cowboy boots, even to work, until they were stolen one night as he slept on the steps of a club. He assisted me with reading matter and apologised for owning only *Red Dwarf* diaries and scripts. He taught me how to use a bookmark and how not to age a book spine, because although his collection was scarce it was precious.

The house we squatted in and they lived in was owned by an Italian called Dominic. He also owned 'Britannia Cafs and Cabs' and within three weeks he gave Jonesy and me jobs as cook and dishwasher/teasmaid. By this time we had also discovered Rock City and spent most of our time there blagging tickets and backstage passes with Camilla (who had a gift for that sort of thing), for bands like Ju Ju Hounds, The Quireboys and GWAR.

Nottingham's resident window-cleaner was called Mad and also cleaned the interior of Rock City. Camilla and I spent nights in Mad's store room looking at photographs of him with Alice Cooper, his band Sic Boys and meeting bands that he'd invited for a drink or a smoke. I slept all day, begged for entry fees with Camilla, danced until four, crossed to the café, worked until nine and went to bed again. Once, on completing a gig, Ugly Kid Joe came in for a steak. Danzig's guitarist asked me for a coffee and Star Star stole some biscuits.

A nose-piercing here and a Concrete Gerbil T-shirt there, I only discovered how unhappy I was still when I started to cry whilst having dry, painful stomach-churning sex with Jonesy, because for once I couldn't avoid it. Because this time all excuses had left me unshielded.

Not even when we were all evacuated from the café because a bomb had been planted in the pub next door had I felt so unprotected.

I had escaped from one tank of repression only by climbing into someone else's.

I had left in October, and Nottingham's Christmas lights had been turned on. I wondered if my mother had realised exactly what she'd had, locked in the bedroom upstairs, now that she had lost it; and I thought about some school friends who told me to wait until summer in case I did have to sleep outside. But I gave up a trip to Radford police station to go and see a Blondie tribute band in the Royal Concert Hall with Sam.

One day two detectives knocked the door with a photograph of me. Jonesy answered and said he didn't recognise her, the red-haired girl with a Batman T-shirt on a boat in the Isle of Man. They left and he said we'd relocate to London soon, then everyone went back to sleep. 'Shouldn't we go now?' I said into the slumbering atmosphere of the room. They had traced us through Jonesy's giros which he was still cashing. Then indifferent to everything I went back to sleep too. The cops came back in an hour with a woman this time, searched the house and barely gave me time to swap addresses with Camilla. The woman followed me to the bathroom and watched me having a piss, in case I climbed through the window. They took Jonesy and me to separate cars; the woman came with me and said, 'Don't bother running in those Doctor Martens, you won't get anywhere.'

'Is that why you're issuing them to prisoners now?' I asked. She didn't know whether to laugh or scowl, and neither did I.

We were supposed to be driven back to Wales in separate cars but I think the Nottingham police misjudged me and out of pity asked us if we'd like to travel together. Jonesy said yes and I shrugged my shoulders. 'Okay then, but you can't tell your parents, Rebecca.'

'Parents'. That's a strange word I thought and then sat empty and blank, with Jonesy's handcuffed arm trying to make its way to mine, throughout the journey. At one point he asked if he could have his cuffs removed and I remember thinking, don't demean yourself any more. And I didn't think again until I saw the 'Welcome to the Rhondda' board on the Bwlch. I'm sure the police driver slowed down passing it, to prolong my displeasure. At least that was one spurty reaction my mind threw to my drooping eyes, but mixed with the rest it was impossible to decipher. And then I killed the confusion by thinking I would make a crap detective, if I couldn't even sort my own feelings.

When I stood in the corridor of Ton Pentre police station, the same one I stood in earlier that year, I met the man in charge of my case. He held a photo of me, patted my nose, held the photo higher and said, 'You looked better without the metal.... Your mother's next door, and she's not a happy bear.'

9

My brother and I loved space. After years cluttered with collections of blue and white china, we both wanted room, room to speak without knocking something over. James had good taste in furniture, but now his house was ugly with claustrophobia, with thoughts and heavy ticking silence. Regret, relief, anger, disgust, curiosity and the search for truth. Everyone had something to say but was too afraid to say it. My mother spoke only to tell me she had moved to a flat in Ystrad. She greeted me inside the police station with hugs and waited until we were outside to use the back of her hands. For once, for the thirty minutes my mother and my brother forced me to stay alert with nothing but sighs, family life was closer than ever. And then my mother produced a piece of paper. 'Dear Diary...' The only extract to survive the fire I lit before I left bore the whole story. Bitter facts scrawled onto a smoke-damaged exercise sheet had the power to change everything, slightly. 'Is this true?' she says. Like I would have taken the time to write something so brutal at the age of ten, for no reason whatsoever. I breathed, a deep fulfiling breath and raise my head. 'Yes... it is.' My cockiness could have suggested that I was completely self-cured. It felt like revenge in itself, announcing that I had been living in the abode of devils for four years while they holidayed and drank and laughed regardless. 'Why didn't you tell me?' she said.

The word 'childhood' causes me to remember fakeness. I feel as though I have never been a child. When I was very young I swore with the knowing, mimicking voice of someone who had spent far too much time in the company of my brother's adolescent friends. When I was growing up, developing pink nipples and my legs grew a peach fuzz which would need soon to be shaved, I thought like an old man. I watched my life with tired eyes, disappearing surely, and waited for it to end with little effort to prolong it. When finally the child was turning into a girl who should have been experimenting with make-up, I was walking a city street at three in the morning.

If I had ever been a child, I was not a child for long, and suddenly when I decided I had always been a grown-up, everyone wanted to give my childhood back.

I was never asked whether I should like to take the child abuse matters to the court. I was never asked whether I should like to have Jonesy charged with abduction. Someone saw fit to answer the questions for me: after all I was still only fourteen years old, and soon to be surrounded by policewomen, police doctors, police nurses, police social workers, barristers and judges.

It began in a social centre on the outskirts of Pontypridd. That is where I would be interviewed, the interview would be recorded and played in the courtroom to shorten my presence at the actual trial. The upholstery was peach and pink with blue and purple stripes. The floor was carpeted with soft toys. The way my mother had made me dress could have made me look like I belonged there, but obviously I didn't feel like it. Beneath a cerise Adidas sweatshirt, empty nose and earholes and a plait, I wondered what the hell difference would social workers asking me if I knew what 'consent' meant, make. What is oral sex? Where exactly did he touch? Where exactly did the liquid go? Did he know about my not starting my period? I tried to answer the questions with a minimal amount of speech. I answered the Jonesy questions with arrogant single words. I didn't want to be there, I didn't have to be, so all the time I stared at the video camera and my mother watched on a monitor upstairs, I wondered why the hell I was there.

Then a doctor and a nurse laid me flat, naked on a board, holding my feet together but my knees apart. They prodded me with various metal instruments and talked about my body as though it had no mind attached. 'Looks like a skin fold to me.'

'Perhaps we should check it anyway.'

'But she hasn't mentioned anal.'

'Mmm, leave it.'

They spoke to my mother before I was let out of the room with the board. She met me at the door, took a deep breath and said, 'Well, you're not a virgin, we know that much.'

When the day of my appearance at Cardiff Crown Court arrived, my mother and I were staying at Martin's house. We missed our train because I insisted on watching the whole ten minutes of Guns n' Roses' *November Rain* on MTV, when we should have already left the house. When we got there a policewoman took us through the back door to the canteen. Up until then my mother had tried to calm me by repeatedly saying 'Don't worry; he'll go down.' She bought me a ham sandwich, but I had already become a vegetarian and couldn't eat anyway.

Because I was a child, I would give evidence through a video-link up, so as not to be intimidated by the accused's face. This meant I would sit in a room at the back of the court where I could only see the judge and the two lawyers. However, the jury, the accused and the public gallery could see me. My room was much the same as the one at the social centre, full of cuddly toys. A woman in a black cloak sat next to me in case I wanted water or to be sick or something. She was overweight, with big red hair.

The judge addressed me, asking if I was all right and ready. 'Yeah,' I said. He kept repeating the question and I kept answering 'Yeah,' until the accused's lawyer said, 'She is saying "Yeah" my Lord. If you were to say "Yes",' he looked at my screen, 'the judge might understand you.'

The questioning began. 'Do you remember the video you made Rebecca?'

'Yes.'

'You said during that interview that your step-father raped you, on an average of twice a week, do you remember saying that?'

'Yes.'

'An average of twice a week for a period of three years, is that right?'

'Yes.'

'So you are telling us that this man raped you three hundred times on average?'

'Yes, if that's what it works out as.'

The judge interrupted the court to inform the lawyers that their wigs must be removed, because they can sometimes frighten child witnesses.

The lawyer working for the accused removed his wig to reveal ginger hair which made his eyes even more black and continued with his horrible line of questioning.

'You say on your video, that the first time your step-father raped you he held you and took your clothes off, do you remember that?'

'Yes.'

'Can you explain "how" he held you and took your clothes off?'

'He held me down and took my clothes off.'

'Yes, how did he do this?'

I struggled. And then, 'It's hard to explain how someone removes your clothes. He held me down and the next thing, my knickers were off.'

'Thank you, m'Lord, that's all for now.'

I had been informed by the police that Brian Williams's lawyer would try to intimidate me. What it all came down to was the fact that all physical evidence my step-father had left inside me had been ruined by the physical evidence Jonesy had left inside me. All the prosecution could go on, was what I said that day, or more to the point what the lawyers got me to say. The woman acting on my behalf worked only with a case file because I was not allowed to meet her, yet my step-father was able to have many long discussions with his ginger man with black eyes. The policeman who arrested my step-father at a Workingmen's Club in Pencaerau, then interviewed him in Aberdare, pronounced him guilty right away because he would answer questions with confidence until the word 'Rebecca' was mentioned, at which he would clam up and shake. However, this policeman, like me, could only sit and watch my hell be thrown to a jury to analyse and hypothesise, as though it was a simple case of mathematics.

'Do you think your mother is jealous of your step-father?' he began again.

'No.' I almost laughed. I could have started to give all the reasons why, but they were all too obvious. Why would my mother be jealous of him?

'I think she is, you see, I think your mother is jealous of your step-father for getting on with his life and finding a new girlfriend.'

At this point I was speechless, thinking, hang on, my mother is the one who asked for a divorce, she is the one cooking steak for a new man and planning a next holiday in Tenerife with him.

'Has your mother told you to say this? She has made up this story because she is jealous, isn't that right Rebecca?'

'No,' I shout.

'There is no concrete evidence available so your mother thinks it is a perfect opportunity for you to say things like this in order to imprison your step-father.'

'No,' I shout, jumping from my seat. The woman with the hair holds my arm but I don't notice because I'm so angry.

'I'm right, aren't I, Rebecca?'

'No.'

'Yes I am, I'm right.'

'No, no, no, no.' I burst into tears, and it has ended. My evidence has been received. The woman with the hair grabs me and pushes my face into her bust in some kind of bear hug. She cries too and says, 'I know what you're going through, my son went through it too.' My mother is at the door with yet another policewoman who says 'You were very good' as though it were an acting audition at which I had excelled. 'He was hard, but you gave as good as you got.'

In the canteen again I could not eat. I drank water and craved a cigarette. I couldn't ask my mother for one because she had no idea I was smoking. It seemed stupid not to reveal such a trivial matter to her, now she knew I had lost my virginity and spent a lot of time in night clubs in Birmingham and Nottingham because witnesses from those places had told the police so. Yet I used to be a good girl who came home from Form 1 Biology lessons saying 'If you saw the video I did today, you would throw those cancer sticks away.' My brother had said similar things before I could walk and now puffed his way through thirty a day. A remnant of respect still lingered for my mother. A kind of grudging respect which is built from fear, and I suppose deep down, unadmittedly I wanted my mother to still love me. Asking for a cigarette could knock the last green bottle off the wall.

I've never felt so frustrated as I did when I sat in the canteen surrounded by police, with my mother holding my shaking hands. It was an outrageous feeling because I hadn't felt such an emotion for a long time, at least not frustration with such force, maybe a long, dowdy, decaying sort of frustration that tried to kill me slowly, but now I wanted to knock the ginger man's black eyes out. How dare he call me a liar, how dare he give the only thing that was truly mine away to false accusations about my mother? I lived through the misery his client caused on my own; nobody else knew. He wounded me and the scars would not heal up. Then the barrister comes along and tells me and the rest of the world it is a story my mother and I have made up because we are jealous of the rapist and his new girlfriend. I know it's not. I have suffered too much to know that it is not. My life of self-obsession, self-loathing and self-destruction proves that it is not, but in a court of law the ginger man who mocked my 'yeahing' can prove it is, by dismissing the child on the screen and speaking a rash last-minute defence plan to people who didn't have to live with my step-father for five years.

My mother, jealous? Didn't these people understand that I never wanted to tell my mother because I didn't want her to feel like I did. Like her daughter was just a dirty piece of flesh with three holes in it. Didn't they know I didn't care whether the accused lived, died or went to jail? Didn't they understand I didn't want to be here telling strangers how my step-father ripped that sweatshirt or how the bathroom lock came to be busted that time? Didn't they know that I was actually trying to forget the unforgettable? Didn't they know that all I wanted to do was shed my dirty skin and step out of myself?

On our way to the station my mother and I walked on the opposite pavement to my step-father and his new girlfriend. My mother was furious at seeing him walk free, and in the same street as us. She mumbled to herself and tried to walk faster but I was slow, as if my feet were cuffed. I was slow like whatever energy I had left had been sapped. We used the same station as the accused. We had to because there was only one station. We got so close to him in the crush and movement of city to valley commuters that at one point I could look into the girlfriend's eyes, a blunt fruitless look which could have meant anything. It could have meant 'look out for your kids' or 'I'd like to kill your boyfriend' or 'you sad, stupid bitch, I wonder if you'll end up stealing plants from your children's school.' But what the look pitifully meant to say was 'I don't usually dress like this'.

The trains arrived, two, Aberdare and Treorchy. One on route to a Pencaerau pub where freedom is served in a pint glass and the other, home to prison.

The following day my mother would stand as a witness and talk about a spilt bottle of baby oil, my silence and numerous other matters which only made sense the night I arrived home from Nottingham. After her evidence and a collection of the accused's character witnesses (who my mother said she had never seen in her life) had given theirs, the jury would be out for three hours before they returned to pronounce Brian Williams not guilty of one count of rape or indecent assault, and yet he had raped me again.

10

The only thing I believed I had sacrificed when I jumped inside the cab of a lorry driver carrying AIDS-infected needles and frozen legs to a Birmingham incinerator, was the only thing I was grateful for on returning to the dumb institutional clutches of the Rhondda. I knotted up my mauve tie and walked into Vincent Page's English class with a copy of *Macbeth* in the air, my nose twitching anxiously in the search for consolation. I would sit my GCSEs and impress my family with nine passes. Page tiptoed up to my desk with a stack of copies of political speeches. Martin Luther King's was on top. He put them down and whispered graciously, 'Welcome back.'

I was surprised slightly by the informed choice of subjects I had made with a pale, void head. I had never noticed before what department I was sitting in or who was teaching what; I simply watched the birds from behind the glass, flying and free. I had chosen art, and English had been compulsory, I remembered those, and made a conscious effort to continue sketching salt and pepper pots any ten minutes I had spare in the café, but then I discovered I had been taking French and could converse a little. And then I found myself in Block 6 embarking on computer and business studies, in case my career as an artist or a poet or a rockstar or a tattooist failed and I had to open a vegetarian sandwich bar, or become a PA or even less, a secretary.

I walked around in my black uniform which should have been navy, and my black tie which should have been mauve and blue and yellow but had all the thread bitten out. I put my nose rings back in.

Joanne and Jolene were my friends. I couldn't remember them ever being there before and I don't recall how they ever came to be there, but all of a sudden a pleasant hit of consciousness smacked me as though I had been searching for a crossword answer all my life and finally found it. I was sitting in the canteen sharing a *Kerrang* magazine with two girls and discussing the ins and outs of Skid Row's new album with them as though I had known them since infants' school; obviously I didn't, because if I had they would have floated away by now. Our conversation was not formal, in fact it was quite personal and I jumped out of myself for a moment to see if it was really me enjoying company, and it looked pretty much as though these girls had managed to step over the arm's length radius I kept marked 'Acquaintanceship only'. And it looked pretty much like I didn't give a shit and was quite happy to let them.

I felt too young, amazingly, to go to pubs and we were too old to go to youth centres and we wouldn't be socially accepted in either, with our leather and our home-made tattoos and our black hair-dye and our nose-chains. So mostly we walked and walked and walked through Treorchy, like we had nowhere to go, which of course we didn't. The insults from blonde girls with luminous orange and green clothes fell like water off a duck's back because we knew more than they ever would, we had something special which nobody else understood so we decided we'd all be best friends forever.

The test of mutual esteem beckoned at a distance only when we discussed the boy at the top of the street. One of us would eventually sleep with the long-haired guy from Joanne's and Jolene's street and each of us was convinced it would be herself. Yet after months of ignorance I realised that this boy didn't want any of us, and my cupid theories became quite tedious. Joanne's and Jolene's must have died at around the same time because one day he moved out and nobody bothered mentioning it.

I wondered often how the chain linked between Joanne and Jolene before they found me, how they looked walking down the street, one six foot and the other four foot without a middle-sized me to even them out. I wondered how the Shakespeare-reading, speedily-maturing Joanne ever laughed at Jolene's Reeves and Mortimer style comedy. I wondered how Jolene, who had chosen cookery as her major simply because she couldn't face anything more mental, had coped with Joanne's ongoing seriousness without me. How did these girls ever manage to speak without the flexibility and understanding of someone like me to stand between them?

I began to feel that maybe I did have something to contribute to somebody, somewhere. I began to feel like I was appreciated by someone, like maybe someone did actually want me around. I belonged for once, somewhere. I belonged with my friends, these real friends that came to me like guardian angels and taught me how to be a teenager. And I began to feel what it is like to appreciate, to be grateful for these people. I knew how it felt then, to want to live and to want to live with other human beings.

Meanwhile, non-communication at my mother's 'Little Palace' was vast. (She called her flat that because Martin had decorated it with plush carpeting and peachy and cornflower-type paint and wallpaper shades). I walked around cautiously, trying not to be heard. I asked for water and I asked to use the bathroom; when there was nobody to ask I crept, not wanting to be caught without asking. I felt like a newly placed homeless kid in a foster carer's home, afraid to say the wrong words in case the carer got the wrong impression. My mother told me numerous times that it was my home but somehow it never was. It was always my mother's 'Little Palace'.

When my mother stayed in Martin's house, I went with her. I obviously couldn't be trusted not to take off again. I could have if I wanted to because when we got to Martin's they'd turn MTV on and drive to some Rhondda Fawr pub as if I could be trusted as long as that particular channel was on. I bought mixed vegetables from the Chinese opposite with twenty pences from Martin's jar instead.

Living in two houses at one time can be quite disorientating. You never feel quite like a whole person, and it's something I had in common with Joanne who was juggled continually between her Treorchy father and grandparents and her Ystrad mother. I was perpetually scared of forgetting something important wherever I went, so I made sure I didn't by carrying a holdall of things I would never need, in case I did need something. One day the inevitable happened. I packed everything I needed for my Business mock GCSE and took it with me to Martin's house, because I would be leaving from there the following morning. I woke up on time and realised I had left my school shoes in Ystrad. I arrived two hours late and failed.

That year, Martin bought my mother a house for her birthday, in the same street as his. She was happy, because she never liked the neighbours in Ystrad, but it seemed like a pointless waste of money because she practically lived with him anyway. In fact, all the time the house was hers she only spent one night there. So really, the house was mine and mine only. I sometimes wondered if it had been part of the plan, buying an extra house so that they didn't have to live with me, as though my relationship with my mother was so disastrous, her boyfriend was willing to fork out thousands to keep us apart.

Hendrefadog is a village with a population of five thousand. It seems since Dare pit closed unknown years before I was born there, unemployment became a fashion which takes too long to die out. Like ski pants, and tennis shirts, clothes which are made popular by fashionable sports, but continue to be worn when sport has become unpopular, worn by middle-aged women who have never been skiing, or given as hand-me-downs to children who have never watched a game of tennis. Like middle-class families who refuse to smash tradition by all becoming doctors one after the other, Hendrefadog teenagers followed their parents to the dole queue, making us a notch lower than working class. My generation, the products of unemployed parents, divorce and downright poverty, tried desperately to find satisfaction in joyriding and class B drugs (which were barely affordable), cider drinking in lanes and underage sex.

Hendrefadog is only a small area of the Rhondda Valley and the remainder, the Treorchy and the Treherbert and the Tonypandy and the Tylorstown areas, were much the same. Those who were employed were only marginally in factory or shop work. Its sorry inhabitants were misled into believing they had a reputation for being very friendly, welcoming people, but after spending a minimal amount of time in English cities, I began to see the Rhondda and its people for what they were. It looked pretty much like we were a bunch of inbreeding hypocrites who were all spouting bullshit about living in the best place in the world, when we'd never been anywhere else to make any sort of comparison. 'Where have you been?' they'd ask on my return, 'You've been to London, have you?' On the mention of Radford or Mansfield or Cannock, it would be, 'Where's that then? I've never heard of that.' Of course you haven't, I don't suppose you've ever crossed the Severn river, have you? Of course not, been too busy all these years, signing on and marrying the boy next door and passing the time of day, being friendly or is that nosey?

I was ashamed suddenly to be someone who sings 'We'll keep a welcome in the hillsides' and then burns down the home of the one we welcomed. I was ashamed to be a troglodyte, a mindless cave-woman wearing blinkers. A sheep who votes Labour because my grandparents did. An ant who follows its tribe around in the dark, under the stone, oblivious to any sort of life outside.

Plans had been made long before I was around, to drown the Rhondda, to pour water down and cover the houses, the forests and keep pouring until the water got to the top of the surrounding mountains. To keep pouring until all the people were gone and the whole of the valley was one big reservoir. What a brilliant fucking idea! Plans were never passed, but if they had been some innocent people could have survived dehydration, and the people who once lived in the valley would have moved elsewhere and been culture shocked into doing something other than shagging sheep.

I began to look at the place of my birth, growth and youth with double vision, one which looked down from above and saw through everyone and everything because I knew I could be bigger, and another type at eye level which accepted these common, common people because I was afraid it was all I would ever be.

I always felt kind of like Alan Bennett, worrying whether I should be speaking properly or being myself, knowing too well that the difference between metropolitan and provincial still exists. As his mother's chance meeting with T.S. Eliot made him ever conscious of his working-class upbringing, my short visits to Nottingham city and Birmingham Bullring would perpetually remind me what a handicap growing up in a place like the Rhondda could be.

Before you had time to worry about what outsiders would think of your accent or your Welsh mannerisms, or your memories of quaint houses stuck together with walls so thin you could hear your neighbours having boring Rhondda missionary-position sex, you would have to worry about what your neighbours thought of you trying to get away from it. I wanted so desperately to shatter the dreams of hometown people who only find respect for you if you give up the fight for originality. But if you stand out like a sore thumb, looking like you're doing better than the next one then someone will knock you down. How can you be the one to make the change in a place where nothing ever changes but the shoes?

Progressively I became what my Rhondda counterparts would call an eccentric, with a love for the bold and the beautiful (only where beauty is in the eye of the beholder). Actually, it was something that had been happening all my life, until suddenly I became proud to be a minority. I spent the early stages of my childhood terrified I was some kind of non-human; then abruptly I turned shit-scared of being ordinary. I wanted to turn the Rhondda heads, I wanted the Rhondda mouths to comment on my clothes, and they did. I wanted the Rhondda people to call me a 'hippie' and a 'punk' and reveal how small their minds were with one word, and they did. I wanted them to think I was a junky, simply because I had a nose-ring; I wanted them to think I sacrificed animals to the devil simply because I wore black all the time, and they did. And I laughed and laughed, loud and uncontrollably, and, if I'm not too busy, I laugh still.

Jeanette Winterson's *Oranges are not the Only Fruit* peeled my eyes open with respect to lesbianism. The image of the girls making love for the first time did something to me – Paul Weller style. It was all so rose-coloured and tender as sex was supposed to be, innocent, uncalculated. Beautiful. No knee to jerk your legs open, there was no stubble there to be forced into your face, it felt so nice, just to read, softly, softest.

I watched women, I watched Madonna, I watched Paula Yates who had begun to present Channel Four's *Big Breakfast* and I watched Naomi Jackson, the maths teacher's daughter who Joanne and I sometimes went out with. These women had shiny hair and soft skin and rounded shapely breasts and I wanted to touch them, lightly, and I wanted to kiss them softly, not suck them like men tended to do and actually thought you wanted them to. I wanted to kiss their bellies and their hip bones. I wanted to give a female pleasure, like I never had. I wanted so much to be a lesbian, to touch a girl in the way a man had never done, but somehow I could never get further than the hip bones.

It all cracked open after mindnumbing confusion into a massive surge of feminism. I discovered LA girl band L7, bought myself a pair of eighteen-hole docs and lived by their lyrics 'She's got so much clit, she don't need no balls'. I kicked my bedroom door a couple of hundred times, and really, honestly, justifiably hated men.

11

I had had a premonition at a much younger age that my life would make a miraculous change for the better at the age of fifteen and forever stay the same.

Papered in flyposters and lopsided, a building called Tonypandy Naval Club stood shamelessly on Pandy Square with the words 'All Hippies Smell' engraved on its wooden front doors. Joanne and I found it in June 1993 when Hull's most hopeful glam rock revivers Rich Rags thought it might be a good idea to find some Welsh fans there. From that particular Saturday night on, we shared the ritual so many churchless, music-orientated, bored valley people did.

Throughout the world teenagers fall into two categories, and although a place as secluded and often immodestly rural as the Rhondda fails to share such universal habits, this one made its way, even to us. The first type is the colourful, driving on their seventeenth birthday, school-prom, sports-captain, Americanised kind and the second (which always is for their disappointed parents, second) are the others, the bookish, with milk-white skin, who are cynical and look for answers in cigarettes and alternative music, as opposed to the acclaimed perfection which the first think can be bought simply with a netball medal or an all-year-round tan. The Naval Club is where the seconds went.

The thing with the Rhondda was the constant lack of choice. Understandably, some people would choose to live as far away as possible from the bustle of nine to five, club opening licences in the city and other hassles a place like London unfortunately offers. However, the Rhondda was neither city nor country; it is

62

a valley made up of towns, and in between you could say, if the rising crime was not so rife, and heroin abuse and calculated murder, building society armed hold-ups and all these things which the city of Cardiff regularly underwent, didn't happen in the valley, but they did, quite often. So, truthfully I could say the place where I grew up is physically as violent and as loud as any metropolitan dwelling, yet mentally the valley could be as compact as a West Virginian out of time and date KKK town. I honestly could not understand or sometimes even want to know how we could actually stand up for the National Anthem and say we were proud to be residents.

It was not only our generation of teenagers who were afraid of the sun and afraid of hockey pitches that went to the Naval Club, but all the alive still generations of seconds with odd musical tastes. The punks whose mohicans had grown out, the mods whose scooters had broken down, the rockers who thought nothing could be as good as pure, original Black Sabbath and Led Zeppelin, all those who belonged to something other than the bore of ordinary eat, sleep, shit, disco existences.

Needless to mention, I took part in many rich conversations there and met what I would have described then as some of the Rhondda's most intriguing characters, musicians and disguised treasures, of whom a couple became my best friends.

Daf was eighteen when I met him, which would have made him only sixteen or seventeen when he lived in Joanne's and Jolene's street. 'Don't I know you from somewhere?' I ask him, impudently.

'Treorchy?' he asks, mockingly. His beauty which is heavily masculine in a 'caught with chocolate around your mouth' childishness mesmerises me so strongly I feel weak and have to hold onto him just to stand up, and in his arms I feel free for a moment, light, as if I am a butterfly who has just escaped her cocoon.

Daf lived and worked in an OAP home with his mother and

brothers in Maerdy, whilst studying 'A' levels at Rhondda College, and being too talented a guitarist to play for Ferndale band, Accidental Homicide. After being shifted around the Rhondda and around alcoholic father's and insincere step-father's houses, he had returned to his annoyingly pedantic mother's flat to cook and clean and baby-sit, as though his mother was incapable of it, which truthfully speaking she was, because mostly she was elsewhere with one or other boyfriend.

I stay with him at weekends, catching a train and a bus which he meets me from. All journey I tap my foot eagerly while Glyn the obese driver, always in a woollen blue sweater, sings to his Status Quo cassettes. I stare at the purple-speckled floor with a force I think will make the wheels turn faster until we arrive in Maerdy.

Daf and I don't talk much at first but we kiss a lot, as a consolation I suppose because sex is the easiest part. The first time I visit him, Christmas 1993 is approaching and we sit on his younger brother's bunk in silence. It's difficult, a situation where I have to express my attraction or my fondness to a human and worse, a man. Because I'm weighed down with troubles caused by the species and with a natural loathing for them, I have never had to. And I never thought about having to, at least not directly. My holding this man's hand resembles only the material my subconscious dares to spew while I am asleep, in the hope that when tomorrow begins, I will not remember what had previously gone on in my mind. In other words, Daf is the stuff dreams are made of and it is impossible to find words which are suitable or even a voice to tell him this. I bite my lip and contrive it by kissing him flatly on the mouth. Before I have time to move away and embarrass myself with even more quiet, he yields and I am safe.

Subsequent to the consumption of a bottle of finest Scotch whisky, Daf's and my 'physical' anniversary would be 1994's New Year's Night. Ecstasy woke me up like some kind of Deborah Harry version of sleeping beauty. I was awake and at the point on the Richter scale which I had always been miles from reaching. Someone turned that stupid goldfish bowl upside down and shook it so hard I rolled around and around until I was dizzy to the point of delighted beyond measure and then I fell out and floated like a feather in a breeze, down, down, down, small and beautiful and landed in Daf's arms, naked and pretty and shaking with pleasure.

This is it, I thought. This is forever, what with having sex for the first time on such a significant date. I'm born, I'm a baby here. This is the start, the beginning of my life, and Daf will look after me forever.

When my mother noticed I was spending weekends away from home she questioned my whereabouts. 'Are you sleeping with him?'

'Oh no, Mam, he sleeps on the sofa,' I said half sarcastically and half attempting a theatrical act, because I wasn't sure before I answered how it was meant to be said. I was bored of arguing and bored with lying.

'Well, knowing you, you probably are, I'll get you on the pill today.'

Leaning against her pristine washing machine later that Wednesday I popped the first red tablet from the packet and then I skipped away with a sweet aftertaste on my tongue.

Winter's cold intensity died gradually as January turned to February but my house got cooler. I noticed it suddenly, returning from Maerdy late one Saturday evening. It was freezing and empty and quiet and however much I increased the volume of the stereo or the television (I only ever used the TV for company) or turned up the heat of the two-bar electric fire I kept next to the bed in my room (which was the only place in the house I used), the house remained in its same sullen state.

I cry because I am hungry and there is never enough food in the house. I spend all my money in the fish-shop outside buying burgers and chips and onion rings and chocolate bars and bottles of cola. And I cry when I am hungry after I have eaten it all and I realise I'm not a vegetarian any more. I'm hungry for music, for books, for inspiration to write poems like I did when I was nine years old, but however much I read or write or listen, I want more. I miss Daf as I have never missed anyone in my life. I miss him more than I missed my mother when I still loved her and I went on holiday with my cleanliness freak Auntie and her children and everyone thought my crying for my mother at night was 'cute'.

I phone Daf and speak to him through the night, but whatever he says is not enough to reassure me I'll be okay until I visit him next. I'm at the point where I love him but won't admit it because I am too scared or too stubborn. I cry when he goes and I phone him again. I phone until everyone has gone to sleep and can't hear the ringing any more.

I must stay at home to revise for forthcoming GCSEs, those examinations which once seemed so important. I am quite happy to do it on Daf's settee while he sees to the old people downstairs, but he refuses because he thinks sex will distract me. I think for awhile that he is seeing someone else and I want to stay with him even more.

I start intruding into my mother's and Martin's house and demanding food so that I can concentrate on studying without starving to death. She gives me old bits of chicken and sausages and cheese and I throw them away on my way home because I don't really want food, I want Daf. I watch the *Crystal Maze* in the evenings hoping it will inject me with some energy and enthusiasm to get through some biology notes. I phone Joanne to know how behind I am and when she tells me she's already onto maths I cry because I'm an academic failure and then I calm myself enough to half-heartedly plough through some literary criticisms of Truman Capote's *In Cold Blood,* and then I cry because every passage I refer to in the book upsets me enough to want to get back to Daf. I go back to my mother's saying I want pain-killers for a headache which is going to kill me. She gives me valium and I stagger back to my house and fall asleep on the floor behind the door.

When June finally came around and I sat in the main hall of Treorchy Comprehensive with my year group awaiting instructions to begin writing on our English Literature papers, I was in a way too over-confident state of mind. I confused positive mental attitude with actually knowing something about Shakespeare's motives. I knew I had, but all I wanted to do was get the bloody things over to get with Daf for the summer. The entire two weeks I spent sitting my GCSEs, one after the other, French oral, French theory, French paper, Mathematics 1, 2, 3, Business database, Business spreadsheet, Business research, supply and demand, Fine Art pencil, Pop Art charcoal, bla, bla, bla, I knew would determine the rest of my future and all I wanted to think about was getting away from school for good, dyeing my hair a wild colour and getting on a train to Maerdy.

Geraint Phillips had once been a Music teacher of mine in form one or form two where I rarely paid attention, but dreamed a lot and once dreamed that he should marry my mother and rescue her from the evils of alcohol. Except I knew now that he was gay and lived in Maerdy and that he was in fact Daf's uncle. And as if enough coincidences hadn't already touched our relationship, Geraint Phillips also happened to supervise my final exam on a Wednesday, June 18, 1994.

I speed through my chemistry paper, write any crap down, passing time instead of answering questions and when I decide I have completed the paper with sixty minutes to spare I watch Geraint Phillips walk back and forth the hall, through the desks and the fifteen-year-old heads you could almost hear thumping with pressure and he looks at me often as though to tell me I have stopped too soon. I tap my nails on the desk as though to tell him, 'You're a bore, I just want to walk out and keep walking until I get to your nephew's flat and make love to him as though I haven't for years on end.'

Later that day I was sitting on Daf's lap in the window of the

Maerdy View flat with atlantic blue hair, watching Geraint Phillips' car pull up at his house opposite.

The first three weeks I am in Daf's flat could not be any more perfect. I'm relieved and serene and happy. It seems I have existed for centuries peering through stained contact lenses that could not be washed clean, then Daf widened my eyes and picked them out. Life became a contradiction in terms, clear and rosy. We talk a lot now, I write lyrics, he writes music, he teaches me a few chords, but we still kiss. We waste long hot days in bed. He gets up and clears last night's debris, cooks big breakfasts and returns before I wake; sometimes he spoon-feeds me. We smoke a lot of pot and it is an effort to dress to sit on the balcony or the bench outside for an hour. I've spent fifteen years for 'that feeling' to go away or 'this situation' to end and now I want to stay 'here' forever. I want to spend eternity in bed with this beautiful, beautiful man.

One day the iguana dies. Daf is completely distraught. He buries it in one of the rockeries behind the ground floor and the old people come up to complain because he is ruining some of the flowers (the flowers are dead). Daf mopes around the rockery for hours. I go down at one point and try to entice him back up to the flat but he just wants to sit and reflect on Iggy's life. I begin to feel an extreme sense of wrong, as if someone very ill is waving at me from far off but I can't get to them and I can't quite make out who it is flapping that big, clumsy, embarrassing hand. 'Is it right to bury a cold-blooded creature in the earth?' I ask myself; 'surely it's not.' And surely it's not right for Daf to sit down there all this time. All this time, he could be up here, with me. Something in my stomach is bursting and running riot and holding me ransom to shout. To shout 'Bring that sad face and long hair of yours up here and pay some attention to *me*.'

Something is desperately wrong. I am jealous of a dead and buried lizard.

The atmosphere is already gloomy. I am disappointed with myself for thinking such rash stuff and Daf is in mourning. To

68

top it, his mother turns up in the ugliest dress of purple and pink velvet ever and she is crying because a group of women in a pub have called her a slag. She wants her bed back so that she can blub over a bottle of Pernod all night. 'Get the fuck away' I want to scream. I want to get up from under the quilt on the settee and walk in and tell her that she is a slag and that this is our flat. This is our bed and we should be in it. Why does everyone want to take the rosiness away? Daf is mine, you understand, mine, mine.

We travel around the country with Accidental Homicide who never seem to be able to get any local gigs because they have such an awful reputation. And this is the way we travel, Daf, I and Accidental Homicide. The band members think I am some sort of Yoko Ono character who is trying to snatch Daf away from them, the other girlfriends are late-twenty-something hairdresser types who don't know whether to frown or laugh at my blue bunches and fishnet stockings. I think Accidental Homicide with their Iron Maiden covers and studded leather jackets are too pathetic to get jealous about. Daf and I laugh at them when we go off to bars and drink Malibu on our own. I get the bollockin' when we arrive at the destination two hours late and Daf can hardly stand. At first I think this is totally unfair but later I start to realise that I quite enjoy seeing Daf ordering more drinks when he knows he should be getting on stage about then. I think of all the times I've hidden pedals and leads on a Sunday morning so that he won't get to rehearsal until later and I can use the time he spends searching to persuade him to stay. All the times I've cringed to have Daf unwrap himself from me and switch his amp on. I think of all the times I've thought about throwing his guitars from the top floor balcony. And I start to think that I really must be one sick, sick bitch because it's all so serious and desperate. No aspect of these actions is meant to be funny or prankish, it's all part of one big, deep life or death need.

I am wholly, completely, totally, and utterly, couldn't be more obsessed with Daf. I am consumed by nothing but his person. I have no diary for this year because I don't want to write any more. I think about him constantly, and I mean constantly. Even when I am with him. When he is in the same room, when we are having sex, I am thinking about him and getting closer to him; when he is inside me I want to get closer. He sleeps inside me because I think if he leaves my body I will lose him. I want sex, even when I least want sex.

I hate his mother because she has known him longer than I have. I hate thinking about him once being attached to her by an umbilical cord. I throw up thinking he could have been inside her stomach. I want to be his mother. I want to be everything female to him. I begin to mistake his love/hate relationship with her for the Oedipus complex and I hate her even more.

One time Daf takes his drunk father who has fallen over a kerb and split open his head to casualty in the middle of the night, and I find an old postcard in a box addressed to him from an old girlfriend called Kirsty who is on holiday in LA. I refrain from clenching it up in my tight fist but I lie hysterical on the bed, in the dark, at the thought of Daf having a past life. I want to kill 'Kirsty'.

When we are having sex again I try to kill Daf instead. I wrap my hands around his neck and squeeze as heavily as I possibly can. He gets all mad and runs to the bathroom, locks himself in and tries to kill himself by drinking bleach. 'Why do you hate me? What have I done to you? I love you like I have never loved anything and you try to kill me,' he says. I cry and bang and scratch on the door until I can't breathe and I can't talk because there's no way I can make Daf believe that I tried to kill him because I love him, and for no other reason. I tried to kill him because I thought that if he was dead there was no way he could ever run away from me. He opens the door when his mouth and throat start to burn agonisingly and I give him some milk. I promise him I won't try to bite his tongue off or strangle him again and he kisses me, even though I have mascara all over my face and my hair is blue and knotted and scary and I'm wheezing because I've cried myself stupid and my eyes are red and big and full of veins, and, well, I look like a typical murderess, a real nuts rock 'n' roll Lady Macbeth and I think 'Jesus, the boy *must* love me.'

The most peculiar thing about this insane affair is not that I am a psychopath who has absolutely no idea how to conduct a relationship, it is that Daf *does* love me. We are young and in love, and amongst all the hysteria which is sometimes so intense guitars end up in hot bubbly baths and clothes end up out of the bedroom window in the rain, we laugh like hyenas and to quote from one of our favourite films we 'fuck like minx' and always, the rays of true love running a smooth course shine through.

12

When my GCSE results arrived late in August my mother was on a Greek or Spanish island with Martin and nobody inquired let alone cared that I had walked away from that damn school with six passes, so Daf and I celebrated with a Chinese meal and a test run of all the possible places love could be made in my mother's house.

I had pretty much finalised the decision to join Daf at Rhondda College to sit my 'A' Levels before I had sat my GCSEs, and so it was solidified: that September I would throw myself into English, Psychology and Art 'A' Levels, whilst eating and taking cigarette breaks and kissing in the corridors and holding hands on the way home with the love of my life.

Myra (Daf's mother) finishes with a boyfriend and comes home again. We take up a single bed in the boys' room, but this time it's permanent. She stays there in our bed for good, venturing out only to ask Daf to go buy some more lager now and again. Because she has taken the TV and the stereo and the phone in there she doesn't need to come out for anything else. All the men that come have keys and go straight to her room. And they walk around naked in the night, looking for the bathroom or the fridge or something.

Meanwhile Daf, Hugh, Daniel and I are sharing this tiny room and Hugh and Daniel won't get up for school in the mornings because they stay awake all night listening to Daf and me stay awake all night. I'm praying that the Thomas family will not finally realise that it's ridiculous to live in this cramped state when one of us has a house all to herself further up the valley.

They do of course, they know all along but Daf won't let them talk about it because we both know we have to spend every minute of the day together and if I move out, we can't. But Myra starts to go ballistic about the hair-dye-stained sink and the blue and green patches of colour on the pink walls where I've leaned when my legs are wrapped around Daf's waist. When she sees a bag or an item of clothing that belongs to me on the floor she pretends to trip over it and tells Daf she's hurt her ankle. One day she walks into the boys' bedroom where I'm lying eating Nutella straight from the jar and she must see something that really pisses her off because she runs out pulling her hair and throwing furniture around. And when Daf comes out of the bathroom wearing a towel she punches him hard in the face.

I decided soon after that I would rather move out than see this obscenity again. Myra would have preferred to punch me, I know it, but instead Daf got the black eye. I got the feeling that it wasn't the only time, and that wasn't the only situation where she got pointlessly violent. I pack my things and cart them back to Hendrefadog, in a vain attempt to spare Daf some of the type of the misery I know quite a lot about.

When I hear the deafening silence again and see my breath in the freezing air, even though it's only September, I don't try to bear it, or try and make it easier by turning on all the electric appliances in the house, I take a sleeping pill or three and snore through the cravings. I steal a valium here and there when I'm in my mother's house and I knock myself out whenever I have obsessive thoughts about Daf. I manage to get to college two and a half days a week and the rest of the time I am either plain out of it, or I am in a heavy doze on my single bed, wearing three layers of clothes. I never think about Daf. Of course I am pleased to see him in art class and at the canteen, but I don't cry any more when he gets on his bus and I get on mine; because I am too busy worrying about having enough painkillers or sleeping tablets or valiums to get me into that wonderful black haze of

73

nothing when I get home. And I always have enough and when I don't, when I've used them all the night before, I find other ways to sleep: like taking ten steps back from the wall and running up to it and smashing my head full force against it.

Sometimes I phone Daf or he phones me, but I start to fall asleep in the middle of our conversations. I wake up with the receiver in my hand twenty-four hours later or I wake up on the kitchen floor or in the passage, because the head-smashing business is happening more and more, since now it takes even more pills, more tablets than I can get my hands on.

I know it's wrong, it feels wrong, just a slight sense of wrong niggling in the pit of my gut, but this is it: it's only slight. Everything is slight because mostly I'm too drugged out to feel anything more than slightly; and on the surface I'm quite happy to be addicted to drugs. My random, ridiculous fits of desperation aren't wasted on any old senseless things; now it's all focused on this magic chalk substance. This is how drug addicts act, and it's okay because it is a problem which is recognised and understood and for the first time in a long time I feel psychologically normal, as if people will understand now why I'm so strange and mood swingy, and irregularly tetchy. It is because I want a tablet or I have taken one, or I am coming down from one, not because I am naturally mentally ill, schizophrenic or plain, boring, clinically depressed.

Amidst the sex and drugs and rock 'n' roll there was a weighty lack of money, which while I was happy and with Daf or while I was asleep and didn't need to buy, I never noticed. Then one Sunday morning I wake up and want chocolate. I have not a penny because I've spent my five pounds pocket money on a bottle of MD 20/20. Yet I want chocolate or any kind of nourishment so much I'm willing to walk down to the shop on the corner and steal some food. I've never stolen anything in my life unless you count a few brass ornaments I hid in my coat from my Gran's house when I was three years old, and was punished severely for. Now, I don't care what sort of sin this is, or who loses money, or even if I get caught. I want food. I am so exhausted with being skint. I am so tired of having to go to my mother's to ask for more money, so that I can get myself some tampons. I am so hungry, yet so full of having to cope without food I am driven to the shop, and driven to put jars of Nutella in my pockets, and driven to hide a pasty in my knee-high boots. Then I buy a packet of crisps with some two and five pences I have searched for under the bed and the settee; and I walk back to the house, undetected. I eat the food and I feel well enough to sketch some house plants for my art portfolio. I am satisfied and guiltless.

I plan my little lifting sprees to the last detail. On a Sunday only the son is in the shop, while the rest of the family stay upstairs and count their money or something. The son is always too busy talking to girls or his friends, or anyone else he invites behind the counter, to spare a glance at the security televisions. So I get my food on a Sunday. A regular occurrence, the Sunday saver.

I perk up enough to make a whole week at college. I rewrite a psychology assignment and get an A instead of a C. I start to work on a fanzine I have been thinking about for six months which is a good groupie guide. I go through my collections of music press to research the thoughts and happenings of groups and groupies. I throw my arms around Daf when I see him in the morning and I kiss and cuddle and giggle with him.

It's a Wednesday and we both have art with Simon, the straighter-than-straight but still probably homosexual lecturer. But I want to be alone with Daf for once, seeing I am sane enough today to enjoy his company. We hide around the college, the gardens, the foyers and the computer suites, just talking and kissing and being young and happy, and in love. We find ourselves crouched up behind the benches at the back of an empty lecture theatre, and before we realise we are having sex on the floor. I have a skirt on because I've run out of clean clothes and Daf is inside me. We look at each other shocked and Daf says 'Fucking hell, what are we doing? What if someone comes in here?' Then we start to laugh, because we haven't had sex for a long time and it has happened so naturally and automatically, we hardly notice. We finish it off and walk out meekly. I am warm and blushing and when I get home I want to work some more.

I begin to see Daf more regularly; he comes up on weekends, or when he can get away from work. He helps me with my fanzine; I interview Accidental Homicide even though they've never had any groupies. I help him with a solo demo he's recording and secretly send copies of it to bands like the Wildhearts who need a guitarist and solo performers who may one day need a guitarist. In the meantime I convince him to set up a student band who are going to be called Cash Money Piggy and I visit the flat and help with his brothers because his mother starts to go AWOL again.

Somewhere along the line Daf gets involved with or dragged into my shoplifting expeditions, and the amount of food and drink that ends up in our possession, free of charge, soon becomes more than we need, more than we will ever consume in a day or three or even a week. But we don't stop, we steal more. We both start getting greedy. Daf gets all these bottles of whisky and Malibu and wine from supermarkets in Treorchy, and brings them to my house. We could sell them and make some cash here, but we drink them all, and it's too much to drink, but we're drunk and we steal more. We hit bookshops and toy shops in Pontypridd, walk out with books and sweets and all this stuff we will never ever need, just for the sheer buzz of getting away with it. We compete. Who can get the most out of this place? I end up with nine bottles of perfume from Boots because the security guard knows Daf from a previous band and I clear the shelf under his nose, while he lies to Daf about getting signed up by Geffen.

When we get home we value it all, and it's like two, three hundred pounds worth of stuff we don't even want. We laugh at all the goods and at ourselves; and we make love surrounded by it all, like some weird Bonnie and Clyde fun-loving criminals.

Joanne invites me out one Sunday evening to a music quiz in Treorchy pub. Because Daf has gone home, I want to go. I want to go out with a friend I have almost forgotten about but come Sunday evening, I have, surprise, surprise, no money. I don't want to look destitute and drinkless when she introduces me to all these friends she has met, while I've been elsewhere, sleeping or making love or eating Nutella.

I'll take my own, steal my own on the way out; and I walk into Treorchy Spar with my leather jacket with eight pockets. I put what I want into my pockets and walk out and then I feel a firm hand on my shoulder. 'Back in,' says the manager, and drags me back through the evening shoppers who stare, into the backrooms, and into the office. The police are informed and the manager tells me to watch the security videos. 'You were good,' he says, 'but not good enough.'

'I bet you say that to all the girls' I say. When the big fat pig comes, he asks me if I'm sorry. 'No,' I say. I'm not sorry. This is not about pride, I have no pride. I'm brassick and this manager owns three shops. I am simply not sorry.

I tell the pig where I live, and tell him that my parents won't be there. He doesn't believe me, so I hand him my union card with my address. Then he asks me what 'A' Levels I'm reading, and I tell him, and he looks completely shocked. He takes me to the car, and it is only there I begin to cry, where the manager with the money can't see me. He says he'll take me to the house, and if there is nobody there, I'll have to wait at the station. And I think, that's great, I'll have to wait there forever and they'll feed me three times a day. Then he asks me if I am crying because I am ashamed of what I have done. 'No,' I spit. 'I'm not sorry, I don't feel guilty and I'm not ashamed. I am just sick to the teeth of not being able to go out and see my friend, or to buy a square meal, of not being able to buy any clothes; and of living on five pounds a week in a house on my own.' I suppose I freaked the man in uniform out because when we got to my house, he let me out and drove off. Probably not wanting to get involved in any social or domestic struggles.

People could say that my shoplifting habits could have been born out of personal troubles, like mental illness, like all my other obsessions: Daf, pain-killers, death, silence, etc. It is well known that women who suffer from bulimia or anorexia often become addicted to shoplifting, stealing size 6 underwear which will not fit them. Yet however much you analyse my need to start stealing material possessions, I know it has little to do with being an abused child, or a neglected teenager; or indeed that it has anything to do with that. I am a sixteen-year-old student living on her own. I steal because I need to. I need to steal, because I can't afford to buy.

13

Griff was the type of person you could easily marry, and never think about having sex with. A person you could describe with the mostly overused 'a genuinely nice bloke', and need no further explanation. Daf's best friend. He lived in Maerdy all his life and still had no idea if the 'e' or the 'a' came first. His mother died when he was fifteen and he'd probably never seen his father. Two brothers had taken off to London and to Bristol to find their fortunes in the dirty smoke. He knew the law and exactly how to break it, without any type of qualification, because he had dealt single-handedly with the council and social security ever since he was left on his own.

One day he announces he's going to visit his eldest brother in Kensington and Daf and I are left in charge of his flat, and his greyhounds, for what he calls a 'few weeks'. His flat is situated in the middle of the old estate, high on Maerdy mountain. A two-roomed brick box, neglected by demolition. Yet Daf and I perceive perfection. There is no heating, so we smother ourselves with foul-smelling sleeping bags on a single mattress, in the corner of the room which is infested with old W.A.S.P. posters.

That morning we found tens of magazine-wrapped sachets on the doormat, which had come through the letter box at some point in the night, from who knows who? Daf grinned wryly at the sight and carefully opened one under our inquisitive faces. A million pink crystals shone, only a little more sparkly under the passage light than Daf's eyes.

'Shall I make some fish finger sandwiches?' I ask.

Daf giggles, 'You won't need them. You won't eat or sleep for two days.'

Forty minutes later a ponderous energy pushes through me, starting at the soles of my feet and hitting the finally concreting tip of my skull. Physical, emotional frenzy. Surely it's not possible to experience ecstasy more favourable than the first time Daf held my hand in Maerdy High Street.

That week I lost five pounds. The following week I had lost ten; in a month I lost one and a half stone. Soon enough, I wholly ceased to eat. The chocolate, and the tuna salads and fluffy cheesecakes that Daf could cook so delightfully, ceased to interest my senses. This was a sure sign, if nothing else, that amphetamine was quickly changing my life.

Daf's ribs and hip bones pressed out of his rotting skin. The skin on my calves changed from a light tan to a deep blue. Veins started to pop out from under my skin, purple red and black. My limbs began to resemble the Cardiff A-Z.

For thirty days the light of day was unknown to us; leaving the house in the sunshine could steal your balance. Everyday I was sick. My mind condoned the drug, my stomach resisted it. Blood and stomach lining ejaculated from my burning throat everytime I opened my mouth to speak. It didn't matter, speed was everything now, my anaesthetic, my diet pill and aphrodisiac.

I appreciate Martin because I know he is the reason my mother eventually filed to divorce Brian. I know they could have gone on drinking and fighting forever, if Martin had not turned up at the Dare Hotel one night, and charmed the barmaid with his Air Force medals and his English gentleman's manner of opening car doors. I know that this man in some distant, unintentional way has saved my life. I remember lying in bed, shivering inside the shell of a pointless black war wreckage and wondering where my mother was. Wondering why she wasn't there to pick me out of this bloody, wet and painful battlefield I have for a child's bed; and I just guessed she was at Martin's, where a trail of underwear led to a bed of roses. It should have made me angry; it made Brian angry. I figure that's actually a large part of why he's hurting me: because my mother is hurting him. But I also figure that he's hurt my mother and she wants to get away as much as I do. The problem is she does get away all the time, but until she announces it's permanent I can't get away once. I pray that Martin will stop opening car and bedroom doors, and will get some real action going; will do something so sensational my mother will come home one morning and announce we are moving out. Of course, years later this is what happens, and I thank Martin for it.

Yet I can't find it, the thing which triggers off the pleasantries of life, love and goodness. I can't find it in me to particularly like him. I suppose in the beginning, I was scared that he would try to rip some life out of me too. But later, it turned out to be just the dead personality, which causes me to dislike most people. I can't help thinking that in the process of saving me, he has stolen my mother, which has actually just made my life a whole lot worse.

I realised my position when I started sobbing out salt water and home truths to the copper who came and got me from Treorchy. I thought, hang on, I really haven't seen my mother for a good few years. She's with him all the time. She lives with him. She cooks him gammon and chilli, and she gives me old scraps to take home and eat on my own, in a house with no gas and little electricity. And while they sit drinking liquor in front of the fire, I am planning how the hell I am going to make it out of a shop with my dinner in my pocket. When they are abroad I'm traipsing back and forth between houses to feed cats and dogs, and water plants; none of which belong to me. And my mother hates the sight of me, because she just wants to forget she has a daughter now and get on with her life; get on with Martin, so that is what she does.

'Do you like Hitler?' Daf asks in an attempt to explain something I find impossible to comprehend.

'No.'

But you must understand that he must've been one great man

81

to have enough power and influence to do what he did, even if you don't like him. That is respect.'

'Don't be so stupid. You sound like a Nazi. Hitler only became Germany's leader because of political circumstance. It has nothing to do with power and influence. The Communist Party broke down and only Hitler was left, that's all.'

'Oh Christ...' Daf says.

At sixteen years old I am a well-read teenager, and I can tell you the meaning of the most obscure poetry and lyrics, if you ask. I know quite a lot, but I do not know and could not explain the concept of 'respect'. It bothers me, it really does, because however many dictionary references I make, however many times Daf explains it, I cannot get my head around it. I don't consider humans in such terms. I either like them or I don't. And the shortlist of likeables is very short. Respect falls into that incomprehensible category along with trust. I might have understood at one point. If I did, it was long gone.

Daf began to find it tedious, all the questioning, so tedious he started to think it was a joke. Like when I used to ask him what a rainbow kiss was, to see if it would embarrass him. He thought I was testing his patience.

I guess I prove him wrong when I copy down the numbers on Martin's credit cards while he's on holiday with my mother; take the expiry dates and copy his signature and then buy clothes by mail order. Boots and L7 T-shirts, jumpers and dungarees, all this stuff which is so cool. It's good to have new clothes, clean clothes. I wish I didn't have to do it. I wish I had money to buy them myself, but I don't because my mother is spending my family allowance benefit on his groceries.

Gradually, what I have of a life, the only real solid foundations that keep me standing, begin to unravel. Daf and I are still in love, and I still know that it's going to be a forever thing, but it is so difficult to keep it running smoothly when his mother has embedded herself between us. I can't stay at Maerdy because there's no room. Daf can't stay with me because he has to work. He's been banned from Griff's flat because it is unhealthy; still I know he has been banned because his mother can't stand to let us be together. And I thought I had a bad case of the green-eyed monster! When Daf and I talk on the phone, he is called away to wash a dish or clean the bath.

Because all this is happening, the only chance I have to see or speak to Daf is at college. I am absent from lectures. I am in the canteen with Daf, or in the corridor with Daf, or on the field with Daf.

I go to the Naval Club with Joanne sometimes but the Naval becomes so glum and empty, nobody goes there any more. People have children and can't get baby-sitters. People move to Cardiff to get away from the God-awful Rhondda and go to Bogiez instead. The custom whittles down week by week, until Joanne, her auntie and I consume the space of one small table; and the staff begin to find it hard to continue opening every Saturday evening.

Joanne's life progressed while mine doted on Daf's. She had spent a lot of time exploring Treorchy night-life and became friends with local bands like Psycho Elliott and Whack Turkey in the Lion and the Prince. I turned to her selfishly when I was left without Daf. But she was willing, quite selflessly, to introduce me, and let me become friends with all these band members and their friends. I interviewed them, researched them and wrote about them for my fanzine; and they helped me with the photocopying costs and free CDs and tickets. My fanzine, entitled *Smack Rupunzel,* was released and sold well. I am pleased with the result, and I am pleased with my new circle of friends. I have socially never been so healthy and yet I can't help thinking I am losing everything. While I clutch onto exciting new straws, the most important ones, the ones I used to have such a tremendous grip of were loosening and slipping away.

When Griff finally returned to Maerdy there was no chance of Daf and I sneaking to the flat any more. I visited his flat for an hour or two on Saturday, and listened to Griff talk about the amazing differences between Kensington and the Rhondda, as though I knew nothing about it. More to his dismay, he had to tell us that his brother ran an amphetamine factory in a block of flats which Griff's neighbour shared. The drugs which Daf and I found one morning were stock which couldn't be sold and was meant to go back to London.

Autumn turned into winter again and Christmas approached. While I am sitting on my own one evening eating stolen chocolate and wrapped up in dirty sheets, Daf opens the door and shouts up the stairs. A 'honey I'm home' type of call and I smile a real genuine smile; and I feel it because it is such a rare occurrence. 'I'm taking you to Cardiff' he says, but kisses me first. He touches my hair and my face, and I feel I am falling again, light and feathery and small. A baby again in Daf's arms. Defenceless and he protects me. We miss three trains and when I realise the time I say, 'You're terrible.'

And Daf says, 'You're too receptive.'

Cardiff city is cheerfully lit with reds, golds and greens. The streets are tight with shoppers, but it doesn't seem to be the usual hustle and bustle of having your feet run over by a trolley or a pram. It's like dancing, consuming the space you have and feeling free with it. It's a film noir-style bubble. That's where we are, Daf and I, floating above the carol singers, being pushed gently along by the notes of 'O come all ye faithful'.

Daf's priority is to get to the late-opening Cranes with intentions of smudging his hands all over the brilliant Korg pedal, new on the market. He chooses a long route whereby we pass a specialist silver jewellers, because he knows I don't like gold. It's a ring with amethyst inset placed on the third finger of my left hand. It is outrageous goodness wrapped around me in twenty quid's worth of metal. It makes me tearful, because it is so beautiful. It's so unrealistically perfect I have to think about it. I think about it too much, I think about how I absolutely detest Christmas, and what a sad time it usually is for me; and I almost regret Daf trying to change that. Then I figure, what the hell? What's done is done, and I throw my arms around him and we circle in each other's arms, round and round and round like this ring.

Approximately three weeks of empty time taught me how relevant material possessions are. A well-known interior designer once said that everything in your home should be either beautiful, functional or both. For a time I tried to live my life by his sentiments and it worked. Of course books and compact discs aren't merely material. They are my most important sources of education, and education of the right sort is power. Power is neither irrelevant nor material.

I kept such a tight cage on my mind, I thought it impossible once that anyone could get in there. I made friends and I fell in love, I made friends and I fell in love, but I sort of thought that everything material is everything you do not get mentally involved with. So however much I appreciated these people, they never came close to education or music or writing or power. And neither did that ring. It didn't really prove that Daf loved me or wanted to marry me. It didn't bring him to me, away from his guitar when I rubbed it or stared at it. And power didn't prove to be very powerful when my material and non-material possessions clashed; when Daf wanted to go home for Christmas. Then I didn't care what I had, material silver or non-material type setting; I just wanted to die for the holiday. Something was wrong. Just so mixed and strewn and messed up and wrong.

Daf's brothers and his mother want him for Christmas, and so do I. It's a problem. He says he'll stay for two days – until Christmas Eve morning, and return after Boxing Day. I want more than this, I deserve more than this. I've learned to block out these three days, as I've learned to block out everything else which could introduce me to some old, painful memory. But suddenly I've forgotten how to do it. I've forgotten because Daf has made me believe I won't ever need to again. He was always going to be there. Our 'who needs you most?' bickerings that evening turned into my first suicide attempt.

While Daf uses the last of the tepid bath water, I collect up all the hidden pills, the ones I haven't used. The ones I hadn't needed while Daf was there. Tens and tens and tens, I'm sure it's going to be enough. I'm so sure I get excited and I can't wait until everyone comes in and finds me dead, and then 'they'll be sorry'. I'm not sure if I even want to die, or if I just want to conk out until Daf gets back, even though he hasn't gone yet. Either way I would like fast relief, so I swallow the pain-killers in handfuls, in big throaty gulps. But it all takes time and Daf is all dripping in the bedroom before I am half done. He breathes noisily and angrily; takes them off me and tries to put his hand in my mouth. What he manages to obtain is thrown from the window onto the wet kitchen roof. I grab his trainers and mumble incoherences which sound remotely like 'You bastard'. Half-dressed and drunk I climb the wall; appearing on the roof, all curled up and stupid, a screwed-up mass of desperation and desolation, gathering the dissolving white patches together like a dish of powdered milk in front of me. And I lap it up from the tiles, retching and swallowing furiously, simultaneously; not wanting to look, or be like this for one more minute.

When I returned to my inky mournful bedroom after walking Daf to the station the following morning, I felt a neurotic urge to contact Joanne sharpish. I needed to know where she would be over Christmas; where I could go and be surrounded by life, in the hope it would bring mine back; the life I knew truthfully only Daf could penetrate. It's just like my old tricks, like when I used to play dead to stay alive, but now it's inside out; now I'm dressing up and socialising the rotten carcass just to make it look alive.

Something dramatic happened when I fell in love with Daf, something bigger than just romance. Something which didn't just involve Daf. My frozen blood melted like coming in from the cold and sitting on the rug by the fire. My muscles came undone and

I moved. I heard my voice. I heard my catty, throaty adult laugh for the first time when Daf began to tell me I was beautiful. And then I started to believe him, and I adopted a haughty sense of owning myself, because I could do all these magical things. And later on I became consumed by my own importance. My ridiculous, obsessional expectancies seemed completely ordinary to me, because I was so happy to notice how much was changing. And what Daf never realised was, it was actually his undesigned doing. Love was too strong an emotion for someone as nauseously cagey as I to deal with. It told me how delicious human interactions can taste, but it showed me how emotionally childlike I am, the deep sour ones still lingering. I want to get married when I don't fit into the bridesmaid dress.

New Year's Night 1995, I slept with the Psycho Elliott guitarist, who felt like a block of ice going into me on a cold bed, in a stranger's house. In the morning, when all I had to show for this killing breach of trust was a hangover, the shards of ice stuck into my insides told me what a fool I was.

Daf found out a day or two later. He read my diary while I made him dinner (probably because I made no attempt to hide it), but I wouldn't have told him straight. He said he was sorry to have to read my things and began to cry. He made love to me and I tasted his tears, warm like blood, landing on my face and in my mouth. It made me feel small and solid, like a lump of plastic coated in flesh. How inhumane I am, I thought. Why is it nothing is ever in harmony for me? Why is it I can love so thickly and hate so heavily and never ever feel it's mutual or balancing out? Why am I so strange?

14

My mother was angrier than Martin, which I didn't really understand, when they walked in one Saturday morning. She slapped my head, and at first I thought she was drunk because she was sporting that blunt, bitchy face which appeared when she'd drunk too much brandy. Then she called me a thief. Martin was polite throughout the entire enquiry, 'You see, Rebecca, it isn't only me you are robbing, it is the banks and shops where you have bought things, it's a very serious crime.' He didn't raise his voice once, which I appreciated, even though it made me feel all the more evil. I sobbed an apologetic gesture which didn't go too far, because Martin came over with the all too sensible 'Tears don't wash with me.' 'What do you want me to do?' my blank face tried to ask. 'You have a brain,' he said, 'use it,' before patting my head and going to wait in the car for my mother. It was then my tears dried, and I got as angry as her, showing my teeth just like her. 'Why did you do it? You know Martin is not a bad bloke,' she said. 'Because,' I scowled 'I don't have any money. Because I don't have any clothes. Because I was thirteen years old when you last bought me anything. It's no excuse for stealing, I know, but I don't see what else I can do.'

My mother requested I pay the money back with my next discretionary education grant, which was a good few months away but in the meantime she bought me a dress, two sizes too small, for Easter.

Daf and I lasted until April, which was basically the end of the college year. Throughout, I felt as though I had stubbed my toe and was suspended in the small amount of non-feeling time you get before realisation hits in and the unbearable pain it brings with it sets in. I tried to outrun the devastation, to hide from the inevitable. Locking your life away from living is bad medicine, it is attempting the impossible and usually there is no end to trying. It's like fucking for virginity.

I sit in the freezing cold house shivering; I've woken up suddenly or I'm about to fall asleep and I hate the place. I miss Daf as I always did; it's just that now I know he's not going to visit; know I'll never see him again. I drink more than ever. I go out. I stagger down to Treorchy and into the pub. I sit with my newfound friends and I drink lager rapidly. I also drink whisky which comes from my mother's house. My friends laugh and I laugh with them, as if everything is okay. Yes, my clothes are colourful and my make-up is nice; and I play pool like any other happy, misspent youth; and nobody knows that inside I'm dead. Inside, my body smells of mortuary and my heart is drying up, getting harder all the time until eventually it will be stone again; like it always was until Daf came along. I feel like a suicide without a note.

When I was lying in the bath one evening, the first bath I would have for at least three weeks, I cut myself, purposely. The bathroom was being re-decorated; for some unknown reason Martin had walked in one Sunday morning and ripped all the wallpaper; reminded me of my life. However many friends I made and laughed with, however many copies of my fanzine I sold, the one thing that mattered had gone away. It was my fault, I ripped it violently away from myself. No thought was required for this situation. I took the blade from the razor, the same disposable razor Daf would have shaved my legs with a couple of months back. I cut wilfully my thighs from side to side, until white skin and clear water had disappeared like everything else. Self-punishment didn't hurt, didn't sting; it felt like relief, like confession. There was blood everywhere, which I was sure hadn't come from me. Had I done it to hurt myself or to prove I was still alive? Whatever the reason it resulted in neither. I continued to mutilate, but when the blade got blunt I knew my suffering had in no way started.

My reaction to causing the break-up was that I had disturbed the hands of fate and my life would suffer eternally. I steered the only chance of happiness I had had out of a fourth floor window. More sleep, drugs and alcohol were the answer, because at the moment I couldn't bear to think about what I had done to Daf and myself.

One evening I was invited to a party, but by the time I left the pub I had forgotten who had invited me, and the address they gave me. It didn't matter much; I followed the other people and the music to 7, Saron Street, Treorchy, and found it. In the process I found some free narcotics. 'Look at that man,' a girl who looked much too young to be wearing such a short skirt said to me, pointing. 'He's smoking a five-pound note through his nose.'

'It's a twenty,' someone said gruffly, handing me the amphetamine.

'Cheers,' I replied effortlessly as though I had expected it. I took two lines, sniffled and proceeded into the next room.

A black mass was curled up on the floor, made to look worse by a fawn carpet, and was talking to the door. I stared at him for a moment and then a combat-clad, blackeyed, long-haired, spaced-out, tattooed male, pulled me up to dance, saying, 'It's just Gareth, he does that all the time.' The strobe light, the black and white flashes of people's arms and legs, the pounding music, the pelmet falling off the window and hitting the stupid girl on the head, gave me the false sense of security I wished I could always live with. I wanted to fall back, and know that one or all of these people I didn't know from Adam would catch me. I knew they would. But they wouldn't, not like D... and I couldn't fall because I was already on the floor, rolling a joint and talking, talking, talking about what to all these people? And smiling so hard, it was beginning to hurt, and I'm talking so much that my mouth begins to froth up; and then I see some of my favourite colours in the next room, and go to them.

I tell some people that my favourite TV programme is *Batman* and I begin to dance again, then someone takes a photograph of me and I talk to them about photography. Then I take the twenty-pound note up again, and then I dance some more, someone touches my neck, I think by accident, and I float like a helium balloon and hit the roof while I'm still talking, talking, speaking. Talk an industrial band called Shatner into taking me on as a lead singer. They say I can if I do a good impression of Bjork, so I carry on talking in an Icelandic accent, and someone hands me a bottle of vodka...

I go to Saron Street every night after the pub, and every night there is a party. Every night there are drugs, and every night there is alcohol. It takes a good two nights before I discover who actually owns the house. I buy my own supplies of speed and cannabis when I can afford it; I take an abundance of paracetamol and diazepam when I can't. The beer makes me put on weight, and I regard each petty temazzi dealer as a personal friend. I live in this stranger's house with all these other strangers and I quite like it.

Sometimes I woke barely sober enough to fathom I had slept with a stranger. I would run to the toilet or the nearest suitable space and sick all the bad medicine and bad action out. I felt so victim-ish and regretful and helpless, I would want to run and hide again. There was nowhere I could run without feeling any worse. I'd hide behind skin, already pierced. No option but to hide in my head which was as terrifying as anywhere else, so I disguised it for myself, from the dingy nightmarish place it mostly and definitely and presently was, to a reasonably merry place, using those crazy big things called alcohol and drugs. Everything brought me back to it, because everything was too awful to witness unintoxicated. The horrifying parts in between which drove me to the nearest bar, are the memories; because all the laughing, the fun, the cheap thrills and happiness which may well have gone on, which my photographs suggest went on while I was drinking, were utterly inconceivable. The memories were the fitting part; the waking up next to strangers who made me sick was the best of the hardest you could be on yourself.

You could hate yourself so much you would put a gun in your mouth in a very non-self-pitying manner, and blow your own head away. Even though you wanted to live, just so you could taste a cold lager pour down your throat, and warm your body to the point of melting and forgetting, one more time. And fuck yourself up all over again. And fuck someone else, and hate yourself passionately all over again. And want to kill yourself all over again. A little different to a razor blade, this punishment worked. Total, utter messing yourself stupid, creating a reputation, a frighteningly dangerous facade, which is worse than how you started out drinking in the first place, just hoping that other people will start to hate you as much as you do yourself. Now, this *is* self-mutilation.

When my summer term grant came through, even though I hadn't been to college for the past two months except to sit a couple of mocks, I paid it into the bank and told my mother it hadn't turned up yet. I kept it there for two weeks, and took it out the evening before I left for the Glastonbury Festival. I dyed my hair bottle-green, especially for the event; and spent most of the weekend not knowing which band I was trying to watch; and thinking every boy who walked past me was Daf with his hair cut, or Daf with his hair bleached, or Daf with new trainers.

Sunstroke, LSD, bad toilets, vomit, and having your friends arrested for pissing in the middle of the main routes; all the things the music press talk about as though they are scenarios which only happen in Somerset towards the end of June, didn't make much difference to the past three months of my life. The only clear reminiscence I, and most of the other people on the bus home come Monday, could possibly make, was Skunk Anansie arriving on stage thirty minutes late, and only being able to perform four songs on Saturday morning. I remember it only because I had made arrangements to watch it with the boys from my band, and because it was a fairly sober, come-downish Saturday morning. When the trim ebony figure known as Skin left the stage, Ray, Stu and I got back to the beer tent.

Back in the South Wales valleys, Lee Chooch and Byron Davies, men I had exchanged pills and greetings with, were taking heroin overdoses and hanging themselves. My mother was on the telephone to Rhondda College enquiring where my grant was. I cried for two days solid on my return, a thick dry gloom working around me, while I let the inside out, periodically. The final attempt my mother made to scream some sort of apology or explanation out of me was made final because I didn't just hide my head and sob about nothing; the type of nothing which really means everything. Not this time. I screamed louder than her 'Leave me alone' and hurled some magazines and papers around the room. I threw my rat's cage at her and pushed her. At which point she fell to the floor voluntarily, to make the damage look worse than it actually was, and I thought 'Seventeen years, seventeen years it has taken me to get half as drunk as her and smack her one back. Seventeen years is a long time. You've done well, Rebecca.'

A few days later I woke on a cold, tiled kitchen floor slightly more soaked than a wet T-shirt competitor. The light from the ceiling blinded my swollen eyes. A dog was eating and the food smelt of the foul routine of living. A Saron Street stranger stood above me, with a shit-coloured bucket hiding their face. A thumping headache, and a pain in my thorax almost prevented me from understanding I had just woken from a paracetamol-induced overdose. I thought of Daf. I usually did on waking, before I proceeded to drink in order to stop thinking about him. This time I thought about how I was borrowing existence from a life machine controlled by him; and how I had taken so much from him already, and yet I was still breathing.

93

Propped above my alarm clock, I kept a photograph of Daf. A distinct black and white print, which made him look, appropriately, as if he'd walked straight out of the pages of *Vogue*. It had been taken outside Rhondda College, where he leaned provocatively against a wall with his hair down and curled from the morning rain. It had been taken during a photography module, when a group of us had gone out to experiment with subjects, and Daf had seemed like the obvious one. I remember lots of photographs of Daf. Sitting in grass with flared Levi's his father had kept from the 70s and string sweater he had borrowed from me. His eighteenth birthday celebrations at the Naval Club, where he had my lipstick all over his face, because he wouldn't stop kissing me. None of them survived our bickering. Daf had a habit of ripping photographs, because he knew they were of sentimental value to me. I had placed the sole survivor in a silver frame my grandparents gave me. It always seemed like a useless gift, until that photograph had been developed.

It meant if I slept in my bedroom and my alarm woke me, I woke to the sight of Daf, as well as the thought. I turned it around at 3 am one night, late in July, because it kept distracting my cleaning of my room. Then I turned it around again because a minute later the room seemed more empty than it usually was. Then I couldn't stop looking at it, so I turned it face down; which made me feel sick. Like when I woke to someone other than that picture, like a film where the lawyer or the psychiatrist puts his photograph of the wife and kids in the drawer when the young female patient enters. I pick it up again and feel relieved. Then I actually look at the subject and I am angry, at what I'm not quite sure, but it makes me hold it up and aim at a wall. This muscle reflex has become compulsive. I began to smash bottles once I had consumed the contents and threw mike stands around at Shatner gigs. Little pieces of agitation and frustration had begun to show through everything I did. I managed to retain the photograph though, just when I was about to let it all go. As I was about to throw away the last detail I knew of Daf, I scared myself into calm. I sat at the foot of the bed with it in my hands, the wet from my face streaked through the lipstick stains on the outer glass. I returned it. When I finished crying I continued vacuuming, red-eyed.

I lost Daf because I drank a lot of whisky, snorted a lot of speed, and was unfaithful to him. Because I was unfaithful to Daf, I drank a lot of whisky and took a mass concoction of drugs, because I wanted to ignore what had happened. Because I spent my entire energy imitating ignorance, I ceased to work. I stopped studying art, English and psychology, and forgot what I had already learned. I could not return to college in September, because all my intelligence had turned to chemical jelly. That photograph was a still which captured my life when I was somebody else.

When I woke at four the following day, I counted my coins, and made for the pub.

15

On Christmas Day 1995, somewhere between 7 and 9 pm, I was sitting in the Lion Hotel, staring at my friend Andrew's new shirt. It was red with black patterns, short sleeves, the most atrocious thing I've ever seen in my life. 'That shirt is awful, man,' I said. 'Oh,' he began, 'I thought it was quite cool.'

I never saw him wear it again. Andrew, or Station as he was known in Treorchy as opposed to Tonypandy where he lived, was my best friend, although I'd never admit to it, partly because of his taste in clothes. He was a member of a local band who I had met in the Naval and later worked with on a fanzine.

The reason I stared instead of drank was simply because my hands were too cold to pick up a pint glass without dropping it. And I'd probably drunk enough already.

My mother had gone on holiday to Crete or perhaps Fuerteventura, so I was staying in her house, feeding the cat. I went to my brother's house for dinner, which I knew would be terrible, because sharing Christmas dinner with people you hardly know is terrible. I hoovered his living room for him and he discovered I smoked, because my fingers were an unattractive nicotine yellow. We drank so much lager that morning, I never really got started on dinner. Cathy took me home around 6 pm, probably because they were going out. And if Station hadn't phoned to tell me to collect my present in the Lion, while sitting on my own, alcohol-less and drunk, watching *Only Fools & Horses* Christmas special, I probably would have staked out the paracetamol.

I almost froze during the long walk down, so it took me a good half an hour next to the radiator, before I could unwrap the present. It was a toy guitar, a baby thing with buttons; when I pressed it it made a widdly-widdly Steve Vai-ish sound. I was getting serious at the time about playing guitar, so Station thought it would make a nice novelty. It did for Coggins, a bloke I knew from virtually every party I'd been to. While we made our way to the next pub, he proceeded to thrust it into passer-bys' faces, and press all the buttons at once, because it was Christmas, of course.

I had completed my first term on a Media, Communication and Production course at Mid Glamorgan Centre of Excellence for Art and Design Technology, which I'd been offered in September. I don't really know how it happened; I suppose I ran out of drink one day and made a phone-call. I still drank, but it must have been a loosening amount, because I began to remember things; like where I was last week, or where I was last night. My hair was red and dreadlocked now, having made its way loudly through the spectrum. I was fat; people say I wasn't, but I was: size fourteen. A strange fourteen, where only my waist and my face were affected. I stopped shagging around gradually; and began, in my sober nine to five hours, to work. Write fanzines, write scripts, make films, make friends with all those people who travelled from all over South Wales to get to this art college on the mountain.

I drank and took drugs in order to forget things; and after a year of living with a fumbling unclear sense of things, it became a relief to start remembering. Not everything was crystal, because I still made a piss-up of every Thursday, Friday and Saturday. But there is a considerable difference between going out on a Wednesday afternoon, drinking until you spew; drinking some more and then waking up in a strange place; to staying in on a Wednesday, having a bath and going to bed with a book, waking up and going to college without the familiar hangover. In fact on Wednesday evenings, I attended 'Smelting Pot' meetings which were part of an unsigned bands charity the council had set up for the local band scene to get easier access to venues and publicity. Station and I produced a fanzine for them, and worked as gig promoters for a while, which helped considerably with contacts for business and otherwise.

There was massive speculation over whether I was a groupie or not; and in some childish mumbling way, I flirted with groupiedom in order to write about it in depth. But I never took its hand. Taking a Courtney Love stance on the subject, I will say I spent a lot of time with musicians, and ended up sleeping with some. It could have gone the same way if I interviewed glassblowers day in, day out.

Remembering things like what you said last night to make Lisa fall to her knees with laughter are important if you remember them. If you don't remember what Suzanne's story was about yesterday, then it is not important; Suzanne was only a face. And that is the sort of thing that makes life mundane: not caring what Suzanne said because you're too worried about your headache.

Drink, like most drugs, never solves anything. It fills the teenage gaps you asked them to, and it in turn asks you to keep using it. In gratitude, you will, only to find that it, perhaps being a little too appreciative, continues to fill gaps; gaps you didn't even know you had. Gaps which are to be filled essentially by sober moments. So when it's gone too far and you need out, you must work backwards, opening each and every yeast-glued gap, and refilling it yourself; it can take years, whereas drink offers to do it in a week. When drinking, you are fooled into thinking you are growing painlessly into an adult, but you are in fact getting smaller, and smaller.

And the big gap, the first one, was what I wanted to forget, and I didn't because what I wanted to forget happened before I started drinking. So when eventually I could call myself a social drinker as opposed to an addict, Daf and I were still broken up. The memories I had were too good to go; and sober now, I savour them, not daring to wonder what would have happened if I had killed them.

98

I found a girl one day, sleeping in my bed, eating what little food I had and wearing what little clothes I had. Minnie is one of these people who emerge from a time in my life when things aren't exactly clear. Like when Joanne and Jolene appeared, they can be quite scary at first because you don't really know how much they know about you. How many times have I got pissed in the presence of this person and blurted out some irreversible whimpers about my disgusting life? More the case with Minnie was 'Well, if she's sleeping naked in my bed and sharing my under-clothes, and her mother is complaining about her being with me, am I actually having a sexual relationship with her?'

The truth was, Minnie was an unlikable girl, four years younger than me with a compulsive lying habit. She stole other people's possessions, which were of no use to her, anxiously craving attention wherever she went, and building a 100 ton reputation with every other man in the South Wales valleys. And I had to admit, as I never could with Station, that I loved her like she was my own sister. There was something about her which no general practitioner could have determined that made me think she actually could have been. Behaviour: identical.

The sex and lies that surrounded her blinded the untrained eye, but those that know real misery can see through a thick layer of earth. All too often innocence is mistaken for disrespect. Inside the armour of ignorance which most people knew to be Minnie, I could see a baby protecting itself from the flying shards of missiles waiting to cut unsuspecting victims of reality. Of course, none of this was instant factual realisation. For a long time I plodded along with Minnie on my arm, not quite knowing why. Embarrassed to be seen with her when my other friends passed by, occasionally pissed off with her bullshit and feet which smelled; but mostly bewildered as to what that heavy chain holding us together was. Gradually I began to understand our personalities were locked in the same cage, often seeming like we were in battle with the rest of mankind. They were the defences which are more likely to hurt than help, and I am quite sure that it was looking at my mirror image that began to draw me out of liquidisation hide and seek.

Station and Minnie. That's pretty much the way things were for a year or so. I loved Station and I loved Minnie. Minnie loved me and hated Station. Station loved me and hated Minnie, yet we practically lived together in my collaged bedroom, the strangest threesome of friendship ever, probably.

16

Whilst being involved with the Smelting Pot, Station and I find particular interest in a sixth-form youth band then called Euphoria, mainly because they're good, enthusiastic and the lead singer is personally involved with Minnie. In April 1996, by which time Euphoria have turned to Gash, Station and I borrow singer Mark and guitarist Will, for a half-arsed attempt of a punk covers band called Alison's Tampon. The day of our first and only gig at Greggson's in Porth, is also the first day of my second year Easter holiday; so Station and I decide to do an all-dayer on Jaguar lager from Tonypandy Gateway. We meet Mark and Will who are specifically kitted out in Manics and Pumpkins shirts, at 8 pm. Then ruin any reputation potential they had with atrocious attempts at 'Pretend we're dead', Hole's 'Miss World' and 'Anarchy in the UK'. I convinced Will to let me stay at his house that night, out of diabolical inebriation, claiming I'd never make the walk home after Ystrad. And he let me. And I remember the moment I sat on his bed while he chose a CD. I picked his Tonypandy Comprehensive tie from a molehill of clothes and held it, the diagonal red, navy and white stripes made me dizzy, made words like 'You really shouldn't be here' run around my head, and then Courtney Love began to sing 'Miss World' three times better than I ever could.

Consequently, somehow, I stay in Will's house until the following Sunday, eating vegetarian cheese on toast, and only using the bathroom while his mother is in work; because amazingly, she hasn't realised I'm there, and that's the way Will wants it.

Mark and Minnie had been doing their damnedest to match-make since the preceding Christmas and the most they managed was a horrific fumbling in the dark pre-New Year, because I was adamant I'd grown out of the school tie, teenage angst, arm-slashing phase. But, mid-March saw me inevitably wanting something I knew I shouldn't want. It was having to share Mark's settee one night, watching a 1950s war film with Will pretending to be a Nazi, which was probably the turning point. It reminded me vaguely of conversations Daf and I had about racism, where he would claim to be a neo-Nazi simply to cause minor rages, built on teasing sore patches. Those conversations were the worst parts of a passionate soul-knitting. And ironically, out of sheer loneliness I swear, though would never admit it to myself, let alone anyone else at the time, the conversation's part two, which began that night with Will's Airwalks in my face, and my elbows welded into his denim thighs, were the best parts of a dawning monster which if called a 'relationship' would be laughable.

Invent a word which describes a man who seems to you so pedantic, possessive and argumentative, that you begin to believe you have actually married the devil, and hell, you've just met William Mylsey. Or Myles his name may have been. And for a moment I wanted to adopt it.

I knew the heaviness, the depth of and the colour of the 4B lead lie I told even before I had opened my mouth. And as confusing as this may sound I said it to defend all my previous lies. When Will and I embark on this mild sexual act, he strongly believes that I am an extremely promiscuous liar. He expects me to go off and sleep with someone else the following day; to protect himself from hurt, makes no bones about openly calling me a slag. I don't even know where his opinions come from, but I imagine they are narrowly based on a close friendship with Minnie. I want to do everything I can to blow these presumptions out of the water, so I say as soon as possible... I love you.

And so, from here on Will and I are stuck together in a ring of guilt, hope, suspicion, misplaced trust and a fingertip of sexual attraction. Each of which is held together with the word 'love' which in itself is a lie.

Will was seriously mentally ill, the result of 'being used', and spending too much time in his bedroom, listening to the Manics' 'Holy Bible'. His reaction to anything which doesn't quite go his way is to slash his arm, chest or shave his hair. I, on this mission to prove myself as being a human with morals, try to take this on as well. It is easy to describe things this way now, but if I was brutally honest, at the time, I would have said, his bottomless pit of problems was the actual attraction. Because God knows, I had my own tucked away in the part of your brain where things go when you want to forget them for the time being.

Very early into this struggle, we plan a trip to Club Metropolitan in Cardiff. Station, Mark, Mark's sister, Minnie, Will and I; only Will doesn't turn up because he feels too ill. Station and I buy a gram of amphetamine, share it; and I go off to dance happily on my own. Then I see someone the spitting image of Daf; and Minnie, who since I have been spending a considerable amount of time at Will's house wants to reverse her match-making tactics, goes and gets us an invitation to a party at his house. We go there instead of to the proposed stay at Mark's sister's. On my way out, I say, 'Please don't tell Will' to Mark. I sleep in Daf lookalike's bed, while he takes the settee and drives me home in the morning. Mark, meanwhile, tells Will.

I go to the pub the following Thursday with Daf's initial tattooed on my stomach. I got the tattoo because the encounter with the Daf lookalike tells me I'm losing all sense of Daf, memory wise; and that it's best to keep him in my gut where I can keep an eye. Will doesn't speak to me, let alone tell me to go away. He gets up to do some solo songs. I cry all the way through. So, he walks home with me. The plan is to talk, but I am silent. As we get close to his house, a middle-aged paralytic geezer follows us, and begins to talk about religion over-enthusiastically. When Will makes a turn for his street, he grabs my hand. 'I can't let you walk with him,' he says. We share his bed, clothed, me in tears, he re-enacting an inquisition officer. As yet I have not told him I am innocent. I already feel I have failed.

Will took that morning off school, and we went to the playground so that he could continue to interview me. 'Why did you tell Mark not to tell me?' Silence. 'He's my best friend, he's bound to tell me so why ask him?' Silence. 'That's really low Rebecca.' Tears. 'Answer me.' Tears. 'Talk to me. Stop crying, look at me, answer me.'

'This is the answer. This is what happens when Mark tells you.'

'Why did you go in the first place? If you care, if you love me, talk to me. What's that D for? People who have tattoos are stupid. We can sort this out, speak to me.'

I just sit dumb as though I can't even hear him. At one point I feel as though I would like to talk, but I can't find the strength to muster the words. Perhaps I am not even looking for it. Naturally, I cry instead, but I hide my face. I've done nothing wrong, but I feel like I've murdered a child. I remember another time in my life when I felt something similar, that prevented me from talking too. But this doesn't compare, this is something else. This is like being trapped in a violent marriage. People tell you to get the hell out and be happier for it, but somehow you just can't do it. I could have walked away, even told him I was guilty, and saved myself a year of pain, but I couldn't do it. Just couldn't stand up, just had to keep crying, and hoping he would stop in a moment and put his arms around me.

Counselling and psychiatric treatment were popular to the point of fashion, then. Will got it every Tuesday. But never, not even when the court case was at hand, did I receive any medical treatment for rape. For rapes, years and years of them. Mainly because my mother used it as a threat. 'Stop crying or I'm phoning for a counsellor,' she would say, when she caught me weeping during the court case week. I don't know why I never let her. She had this way of making me say 'No, I'll be okay in a minute' and force back the tears. I didn't want to disgrace her anymore, I suppose. After all, she comes from an era where mental health and treatments for it were taboo, and in her mind they very much still are. So I soldiered on, deadened everything, put the past to rest. Only it never rested, it always showed itself in a dream or in a sick pub joke, or on particularly lonely nights, in a particularly lonely house. So I deadened myself with denial and drugs, until one day I decide I'd like to be normal and happy and find myself a boyfriend. And here I am, sober and face to face with it. Weak, innocent victim, fallen into a defenceless situation caused by another's trouble and grief and bullying.

Will wanted security. He wanted me to be a padlock which held him together, and resisted anyone else's key. I'm not metal, I'm human, often I've felt inhuman, but it was plastic, never anything as solid as stainless steel. I was faithful as faithful can be. I always was, yet Will still wanted more; kept questioning, asking, wanting, demanding. I told him I never slept with that boy. Wasn't good enough. 'Why did I go?' He reminded me of someone. Wasn't good enough. That day he did stop and put his arms around me. He went to school and I went home, opened my arms with a blade, let out everything I should have in the playground.

I don't remember going out at all between March '96 and January '97. Every spare moment I had was spent in Will's bedroom. Watching television or listening to the Smashing Pumpkins. No *Have I Got News For You* because he thought I had a thing for Angus Deayton. I did. I had my friends tape it, and I'd watch it in college during lunch. I couldn't read. That was ignorant. I put a whole load of weight on, because there wasn't much to do but eat vast amounts of crisps and chocolate. Had a lot of sex, out of boredom mainly; but Will thought it unnatural and wondered how I managed without, on a weekday. I arrived late one evening, because I'd stayed back to sort out some fanzine contacts. I'd been on the telephone, taking numbers and whilst waiting for people to answer, I'd scribbled some doodles onto the page. When I kissed Will on arrival, he'd put his hands into my arse pocket and found a Post-it note with a name and number on it, hearts drawn all around. Ructions. 'Sloe Gin Fizzy', name of band, he thought club, 'Kevin', name of guitarist, he thought date. Serious stuff.

Next to the telephone in his bedroom sat a doll he'd christened Rebecca. If I didn't talk enough on the phone, or say the right things to him, he put a pin in it. I never felt any pain, but it hurt none the less. One day I threw the doll across the room; and then he threw me. Even more serious. I was afraid of him at this point. Afraid to stay and afraid to go.

I cut myself a lot at home. Will did that too. Will reintroduced me to it in more ways than one. A night with him was worth a stitch or two. My mother found quite a lot of blood in the house one day, and ordered me to go and live with her and Martin. Just like that. Robbery and drugs and promiscuity just wasn't enough before; but first sight of blood and she's weak at her knees. Warm water, clean clothes, food on table, it didn't bother me. Argument here and there, I've lived there ever since.

I spent my eighteenth birthday stranded with Will on Porthcawl beach. We caught a bus and missed the last one home, spent what little money we had on doughnuts and vodka to keep us warm; had to wait for his father to pick us up in the morning. I was scared, scared even to buy vodka on my eighteenth birthday, when I'd been drinking since fourteen. I thought about being fourteen and running away to Nottingham, and now I was too timid to spend the night in Porthcawl, only twenty-five miles away from home. Something was definitely changing.

By August I'd stopped sneaking Angus Deayton into college, because I was scared Will would walk in and catch me. I dreamed one night that he'd bugged me, and could hear every word I said in college or elsewhere for that matter, and I never really woke up. Instead, always half believed he could, and stopped talking about or listening to Angus Deayton.

He took so much away from me with his demands and his questions, he stripped me bare. First to go was my hair colour, then he took my clothes, changed my underwear. Changed it all to cotton and floral, because only sluts wear black silk. Then he began his one-man, brainwash crusade, and slowly chiselled away my personality. Laid my soul out flat and kicked all movement out. He made me speak, made me tell him why I didn't like to speak, ironed every crease in my life-story. He ripped things away from me and boiled them into condensation.

He knew what he was doing, or perhaps it only seemed like that because I didn't. I hated it. Hated what started with 'Why are you so fucked up?' I didn't understand where the turmoil it caused to explain could take anyone. In my mind, all we were trying to do was make the best of a disastrous love affair, and we didn't need to drag any psychology shit up to make it worse. Will had other ideas and I don't think I'll ever know what they were.

It hurts you, having your life shredded up in front of you, like having your eyeballs ripped out and being able to see outside your face. You're watching fading memories of yourself disappear over the horizon, as you say 'I'll never take another grain of speed.' Okay, I know drug addiction is not the sort of sensible code of living you should hold onto, but when it's all the personality you've ever really had, it's a bit of a bummer having to say goodbye to it. It's painful to realise you're becoming someone you're not.

Will was beating me down, taking everything my name ever stood for. He took all my energy away. Took my life, threw all my memories to ruination. 'You're killing me,' he'd say if someone told a joke which rocked him to weakness. No, he was killing me, I was being shaped by a man-made mould. Something he could take out and mess around with here and there; plasticine. And still I wouldn't walk. Still I kept on giving. Between the blood I drained in the bath, and the feelings I gave away, I was quickly becoming hollow.

I saw many parallels between Will and my step-father. Will was raping me, emotionally, over and over and over. Stealing things which were rightly mine, and I never told anyone. I was afraid to, afraid people would think I was insane. Afraid like so many abused children, that deep down it was my fault, that deep down I was a bad little girl who deserved it. And the hate I harboured secretly for Will he took, took, took, equalled the hate I felt for my step-father for so many years, while he took, took, took. One day, I dreamt about driving to Aberdare with a sawn-off and the next I didn't. The next day I just wanted Will to stop and put his arms around me.

He never did. He kept on taking, until Christmas Eve 1996, when he took the only part left. He took the life I had built to serving his every need.

The argument was really silly. He didn't like the boots my mother bought me, and wouldn't let me go Christmas shopping in them. He told me to go home and never come back.

Anyone who has woken after spending the whole night with their arm under the whole weight of their body, will know the meaning of the words 'numb' and 'dead-weight'. Now imagine each limb and each organ of your body feeling the same way, and you're slightly closer to the way I felt and spent that Christmas. I watched Angus Deayton bring in 1997 on BBC television, yet I don't think a word registered.

17

Adjusting to living with my mother and Martin was both simple and difficult. Simple because I knew where the cutlery was kept, and simple because I knew which bedrooms were which. Difficult, because I discovered what a stranger my mother actually was. Difficult, because she wasn't the person I always thought she was. Yet, nothing had changed. She still loved her drink, still loved her Country and Western, but she was older, and I wasn't afraid of her any more. I watched her dress up and go out with Martin, just like she always did. But more than anything, I wanted her to, because the sight of her ageing face upset me. It upset me so, to look down on an arthritic woman whose sad mumblings now meant nothing, but had once sent me to my room in tears. The beautiful, powerful, frightening Cruella DeVille-like image I had conjured of her was gone, and left only a dying-breed Emmerdale fan, who thought HIV sufferers should all be put on a sectioned off mountain top.

Time left my mother behind, and I didn't like it at all. It was the only thing powerful enough to make me want to be a child again. After 10 pm and a lot of whisky, she'd pour out to me the guilt and grief she felt for everything I'd been through. 'I'm sorry, I'm sorry, I'm sorry, I should have been there' but it always ended with 'but you should have told me,' thereby eliminating any self-recrimination. Still, that meant nothing to me now. I was too confused and too numb to remember anything, let alone blame anyone for it. So I'd just put some Dolly Parton on and ask her to dance; a bit like when I was a baby, only now I feel like the mother.

My Gran was dying of cancer; we had known for a while. My mother came into the bedroom of the old house one morning, gave me a cigarette and told me. Will pretended to sleep, so he could go on thinking he was the only one in the world with problems. She went into hospital to get it sorted, only it never was. She had three operations and each one made her weaker. We knew now, she really was dying. The doctors couldn't give her a month.

I'd planned to spend Christmas Day with her because we knew it would surely be her last; I couldn't though. I spent the day reading. Reading and reading, yet not seeing any words. When New Year was over my Gran needed someone to care for her overnight. The family asked me if I'd do it until I had to return to college. And grudgingly I agreed.

The first night was horrific, not because I felt any sadness or sense of loss, but because I felt like a night nurse unsympathetically watching a stranger, left on her own to die. When I made her toast in the morning from a fine cob, with an inch of melting butter, and she asked me if I had buttered it, I didn't cry because my own Gran was losing her mind, I said, 'Of course there's butter, Nan' and returned to the kitchen to wash the dishes. More than anything, I was jealous. I was jealous of my Gran because she was dying and I wanted to. She, with a healthy appetite and a house full of possessions and a lifetime of riveting war stories, sticking together through poverty stories, marrying, nurturing four children and even more grandchildren stories and she was dying. And me, me with not even a thought in my head, was living. Just didn't seem right.

My grandmother was a strong woman. She had worked all her life. Born in Carmarthen, she left for London at fourteen to marry. She worked through the war, driving buses, driving troops around Britain, and was the only woman in the district to do so. She moved to the Rhondda when she met my grandfather, and she cleaned every pub in Treorchy. Her children were the best fed and dressed; and they were the first family in the Rhondda with a television and a car. My grandmother was a fine woman, and she was a fine woman up until the minute she died. She told me I had first pick of the wardrobe, and she told me I could have her sewing machine, the only thing she owned with any sentimental value. She told me what hymns she wanted sung at her funeral; and she told me she had to wait until the following Tuesday to die, because the Salvation Army have a busy schedule on a weekend, and didn't want to be burying her as well.

Just didn't seem right. Wrong that she should die, and wrong that I should live. I'm half-dead anyway, walking around with all my credentials having disappeared. It seemed like it was only the biology aspect left. And my Gran, well, the biology aspect of her life was getting thinner and thinner, and yet judging by the stories she told me, stories, she said, she never told anyone else, her mind and her emotions were getting deeper and deeper. And it just didn't seem at all right.

The same day, early in the evening, in the midst of preparing to return to my grandmother's house, I tried to kill myself with a paracetamol soup. It wasn't the outcome of a long-thought-out master plan, really, it was nothing at all. I plaited my hair on either side in front of my mirror and still a muscle-aching fifteen minutes effort did little for my reflection. So off I went to mix up a cocktail, as naturally as picking up my night bag and making off down the road. I cannot explain my actions, because although I remember the minutes leading up to it quite clearly, no train of thought accompanied them. It just happened, as if every other part of me had mysteriously floated away from what I now called 'me' and the walking, talking, toast-making bit was inevitably destined to follow.

There were partial glimpses of my brother, of vomit, of saltwater and of my mother expressing disgust on my grandmother's behalf, before I really did die.

The following day I was back at my Gran's house, cooking chicken for a salad, making tea for people who'd come to say goodbye, yet spent hours avoiding the word. And when they'd all gone, Rose and her granddaughter drank whisky together and toasted the coming of new life, secretly to themselves. For my head was now filled with possibilities. A choice of University, and finally getting the driving licence which was talked about so much in some other 'think don't do' place. Maybe some charity work in the soup kitchens of New York; or perhaps a novel about some more unfortunate being who lived their life in a water container.

I felt much the same about my grandmother, realising she was my Gran who I very much loved and respected, but with all jealousy flushed out by a pain-killing drug, my emotion was practical. I wanted her to die as soon as possible, thereby eliminating as much pain as possible. I wanted her to move quietly on to a better place, the happy place she so believed in; the painless place she so deserved to live in. And as I grew more ready to take on the world, like a shell of a Ford built up to be a Mercedes, my Gran grew more ready to leave it. My Gran died the following Tuesday as planned, yet she gave me more than a choice of clothes and a sewing machine, she gave me the person who is writing this sentence. She gave me treasured stories and examples and standards to live by, reasons to fight my way to where I want to go. Reasons to get up in the morning and make the day a success. She gave me a reason to think myself a good, worthy person, if only I do half as much as she did with her life. She equipped me with everything I would need to begin a new forceful life of my own making. The strongest woman I have ever known handed out to me her gift-wrapped strength.

Broadcaster and journalist Carolyn Hitt was born in Llwynypia, Rhondda and read English at Oxford University. She is a television and radio producer, an award-winning newspaper columnist and the author of two books on Welsh sport and culture.

Bronwen Lewis is an artist and singer song-writer from south Wales. She studied at Saint Martin's College, London and her first album, *Home* was released in 2016. She also appeared in the film, *Pride*.